Taking the Ice

ICE COLD SUMMER

Allye M. Ritt

ISBN 979-8-88644-576-3 (Paperback)
ISBN 979-8-88644-577-0 (Digital)

Covenant Books
11661 Hwy 707
Murrells Inlet, SC 29576
www.covenantbooks.com

CHAPTER 1

Again!

Man, it's cold in this rink compared to the summer heat! It feels good, but my body wasn't expecting the drastic temperature change after a long weekend in the sun. But I'll take the frigid ice any day over the humidity of a Wisconsin summer.

"Khalli!" Coach Marie skates over to me excitedly. "Good morning! Today's the day—are you ready?"

It's Monday, June 7, my first day of summer ice, and we are finally starting the Axel on ice! I've been working at it off-ice for a couple of months; it was such a struggle to make my air position look the way my coach wants it. Naturally, I wanted to pull my knees up to my chest and cannonball myself into the air, which is completely wrong! So even though I was fully rotating the jump (one-and-a-half total rotations!), Coach Marie said I had to fix my air position before she'd let me put it on the ice. I think she knew that having to wait until it was correct would fiercely motivate me. I've been doing Axels in my second-floor bedroom nonstop; my parents aren't exactly thrilled by the loud thuds. I wonder why...

But I've got it now, and if Coach Marie says I'm ready to try it on the ice, then I best believe I'm ready. She's strict!

We start from a standstill. "Would you like a pair of knee pads?" my coach offers. "We unfortunately don't have a jump harness at Berger Lake, but if you're willing to drive an hour, we could definitely put you in the harness at another rink to make the falls more gentle."

I shake my head. "I'd love to try to land it without the harness, and I don't think I need kneepads. Now that I'm used to it, falling doesn't really hurt anymore."

"All right, let's do this!" Coach Marie walks me through everything that she's talked about over and over while we've worked on these off-ice. Then we do a couple of walk-throughs on the ice, which we've been working on for the last week. The walk-through is basically a waltz jump with a backspin tied into the landing. Pretty easy, but a good way to remind myself of the little things, especially my right shoulder which I need to keep back.

"Make sure your right foot climbs forward as well, not just your knee," Coach Marie tells me.

I try a couple more walk-throughs, making sure to use the technique my coach demands.

"Good, Khalli! One more!"

I focus for twenty seconds on everything I need to do, and then *up!*

"Not quite. You rounded your take off. You need to jump up and out, not around, One more"

I process what my body needs to do, and up!

"Closer." Coach Marie gives me another correction. "One more."

I should know by now that "one more" never actually means just one more. But I'm not going to point that out to Coach Marie!

I do it again. And again.

"Nice, Khalli. That was three clean walk-throughs in a row. It's time!"

Time? Like...Axel time? I know exactly what Coach Marie means, but suddenly I question if I'm ready.

I don't say anything, but Coach Marie can sense my anxiety. "Khalli, how long have you been wanting to start your Axel?"

"For months. Since spring break," I respond.

"And when you've asked to try it on the ice, what did I say?"

"You said I wasn't ready yet. That my air position would make it too difficult, and it would be unsafe on the ice."

"Correct. You were not ready. We are starting today because you've shown me you are prepared. I will not have you try things I don't feel you're ready for. So if I'm telling you to jump, know that I truly believe that you are ready and this is safe. So it's time to jump!"

It's hard to say no to that logic.

"Okay." I smile unsurely. "I'll try."

Coach Marie talks me through everything again. We are starting this jump from a standstill, which makes me feel a little safer. I land nearly all of them fully rotated off-ice, so why shouldn't I be able to do it on the ice?

I set myself up. Bending into my knees and ankles, I push forward. My right knee drives upward as I launch forward from my left outside edge up to my toe. I snap my weight over my right side and panic! I burst out of my jump, arms opening and legs sprawling wildly. Toe pick first, I hit the ice facing forward, crashing face-first toward the ice. *Bam!* My right hand slaps the ice as I break my fall.

I'm okay. I repeat to myself three times before I actually believe it. I glance up to Coach Marie. Her lips are pursed, head cocked to the side, and she's giving me her you-know-better-than-that look. I bailed. I should never bail!

"Don't tell me. I know what I did. I can fix it. Please let me try again."

Coach Marie says as little as possible as I set myself up to try again. And again. And again.

CHAPTER 2

The End of an Era

Last week Thursday, we had our final day of school. My very last day of elementary school! I'm officially a middle schooler! We celebrated pretty hard on our last day since we'll never be back with our same class or in the same building all together ever again.

Mrs. Hill brought in three cakes! A chocolate cake with the gooiest, most delicious frosting ever! A vanilla cake with a creamy custard filling and pastel rainbow sprinkles! And a small dairy-free, gluten-free cake for two of my classmates who have allergies. I love that she thought of everyone!

We had a party with the delicious cakes and tons of food; went outside to play kickball; played some of our favorite games in the classroom, like heads up seven up and hangman; and then wrapped up the day with a yearbook social.

Because I won't see everyone next school year, I tried to get everyone to sign my yearbook. Berger Lake has two different middle schools: Washington and Lincoln. We get to choose which school we are going to attend, but that means half of my classmates won't be at my school again next year.

Choosing the right school is a difficult decision, as Lincoln has a brand-new pool and a theater inside as well as a fantastic music program; but Washington has an intensive athletic program and a ropes course as well as a lot of artistic programming—including dance—and a later start time in the morning. A later start time means I get to skate a little bit longer before school. Washington is closer to my house, but Lincoln is closer to the rink.

In addition to looking at the schools, it's also really important to me to be at the same school as my friends. Becky's parents decided she would go to Washington so she can walk to school. Becky really wanted to participate in the theater program at Lincoln, but Auntie Liz works irregular hours and can't always guarantee a ride; so being able to walk is important. Dacia is still deciding but wants to go to Lincoln so she can join the swim team. It's looking like whichever school I go to, I will likely not get to see one of my best friends regularly. It's so disappointing.

Because of this, making the most out of my yearbook social and last day of school is a super big deal!

"Please write me a note. Don't just sign your name!" I begged after Gio wrote, "Peace Out! Gio."

"You girls are so sentimental." He laughed but obliged anyway. I waited to read everyone's notes until after school; I wanted to be able to sit down with my yearbook and fully take in some of the final goodbyes. And, man, were there some meaningful notes!

*****

After the school day ended, we had a big party at Becky's house. And when I say big, I mean *extra big!* Auntie Liz agreed to a sleepover party with all of us! Becky, Dacia, Tanja, Keeloni, and me. The five of us got closer and closer the last month of school, and now that we are one big group of friends, I'm really sad to see things change. Both Keeloni and Tanja will be going to Lincoln next year. It's closer to their homes, but they also both want to join the theater.

"Please come to Washington!" Becky begs me at her sleepover after Keeloni announced that both she and Tanja will be attending Lincoln. "Otherwise, I'm not going to have any friends there."

"I like that they have dance. Coach Marie keeps encouraging me to take classes to help my skating. She's having me take a class at the rink this summer. And I like that Washington starts twenty-five minutes later. That means I can skate longer. But Lincoln is closer to the rink, so I need to see how much of a difference that will make. I think my parents want me to go to Washington, but we'll see."

"I'm going to bake your parents cookies shaped like George Washington to convince them!" Becky jokes.

"Shape them like his wig!" Dacia giggles.

"Do you know George Washington actually didn't wear a wig?" Keeloni chimes in. "It was the fashion during his time, but he kept his own hair. Although, he powdered it white, you know, for fashion."

"How do you know this?" Dacia asks, baffled.

Tanja puffs her lips laughingly. "*Pff!* Don't even ask! That girl knows the strangest things, but that's why I love her!"

"Maybe just sprinkle powdered sugar on the cookies to symbolize George's hair." Dacia snarks.

"Now we're on a first-name basis with the first president?" I laugh.

"That's a great plan!" Becky quips back at Dacia, cutting me off. "Khalli, I'm going to make your parents powdered George-head cookies. I'm calling them powdered hairies!"

"That's disgusting! If you bring those to my parents, they are going to send me to Lincoln just to avoid having to eat them!" I laugh. "Thanks for the dandruff cookies, Becky!" I say in my best impression of Dad. "They aren't going to try them, but I promise I will because you're my best friend."

"All right, all right. I'll come up with a better name. Whatever it takes to get you at Washington Middle School with me!"

Later that afternoon, we played truth or dare; it turns out Tanja is deathly afraid of spiders, and Dacia made her touch a daddy longlegs! I nearly died laughing at her face as Dacia put it closer and closer to Tanja's finger.

"You're so mean!" Keeloni stands up for her best friend. "I'm totally picking truth!"

Afterwards, we took a walk around the neighborhood and picked up sticks to use to start our bonfire. Then we struggled to set up a tent in Becky's backyard. Auntie Liz said a five-girl sleepover sounds like more fun than she wants to hear in the house. I'm sure she's right.

"You have to put the poles together first!" Becky laughs as Keeloni tries to lift the tent with the strings.

"Give me a break. I've never set up a tent before!"

"Wait, what!?" Becky and I shout at the exact same time.

"Yeah, my parents have never kicked me out to the back-yard before." Keeloni laughs. "I don't know what kind of fun you guys typically have that's getting you booted from the house to the backyard, but I can't wait to find out!"

Becky, Dacia, and I exchange knowing glances and burst into giggles. We definitely know how to have a good time, that's for sure!

Auntie Liz came outside to put out our bonfire around midnight and gave us a couple of lanterns for our tent. "I'd wish you sweet dreams, but after as many sugary s'mores as you just ate"—she holds up the empty marshmallow and Hershey's packaging—"it's clear you're not sleeping. And I made the right decision kicking you out to the backyard. Now don't wake the neighbors!"

And with that, she heads inside, and we have the best last night of elementary school anyone could ever have!

As I fall asleep when the sun starts coming up, I can't help but smile. I can't believe elementary school is already over. But seeing how fast it went and how much I accomplished, it's clear that with work, I can make my dreams come true! And that's exactly what I intend to do. This summer, it's time to work!

CHAPTER 3

The New Girl

"Line up! Let's go! Everyone to the goal line!" Coach Marie yells.

It's on-ice power class at Berger Lake Ice Center, and Coach Marie is not messing around.

"You will end this summer stronger than you started it. I have expectations, and you will all meet them! You will be sore tomorrow. If you are not, you didn't work hard enough today."

I've learned never to doubt Coach Marie. This is going to be intense!

I look around me. Most of the skaters I already know. Yana, Stacy, Tamerah, Thomas, Coach Jessica, some other skaters from Berger Lake Ice Center, and one new girl who doesn't seem to know anyone but is very focused.

Coach Marie pushes us hard for thirty full minutes. Drills, edge skills, power pulls, spirals, and lunges over and over until my legs are shaking. The rink is freezing today, but every single one of us is dripping in sweat.

"All right! Nice work! We are going to stretch for the remaining five minutes, and then you are free to get off the ice and complain about me," my coach jokes.

Oh, I will, I think to myself.

*****

Once we get to the lobby, I see the new girl sitting by herself. I pick up my bag and go to sit down next to her. It meant so much to me how Yana reached out when I was new to practice sessions, so I'd like to do the same for this girl.

"Hi, I'm Khalli!" I reach my sweaty hand out.

The new girl looks up at me. "Okay."

"What's your name?" I ask, trying to be friendly.

"Mila."

"It's nice to meet you, Mila. You're new here, right?"

"Obviously."

I'm not sure if Mila is shy or just hates me already. I sit quietly, taking my skates off as I think about what else I can say.

"What are you working on? Do you test?"

Mila looks up. "I'm working on my sixth Skating Skills test and my double loop. I came here because I needed a higher-level coach. I'm the best at my rink."

"That's cool." I smile. "That means you're almost the same level as Yana! She's a beautiful skater. Have you met her yet?"

"Mm."

"She's over there." I point as I continue talking. "She's so nice too. You'll love her."

"Mm-hmm."

"Who are you going to be working with here? I work with Coach Marie and Coach Jessica."

"Listen, Khalli. I'm not here to make friends. I'm just here to skate. Like I said, where I come from, I'm the best. I'll tolerate you because it's clear you're a much lower-level skater than me, so that means you'll never be my competition. I'm not friends with my competition. Yana and I used to compete against each other. She passed me recently because her coach was better than mine, but now I'm working with her coach too. I'm a stronger skater, and I am prepared to prove it. Mark my words: by the end of this summer, I'll be the best skater at this rink too."

"Doubt it. Have you met Jessica?" I ask with a calm smirk and turn to walk away. I don't know who Mila is, but she's not going to mess with my rink family!

CHAPTER 4

Working through the Pain

Goodness, am I ever sore! I mope around the house all morning, trying to move as little as possible. Coach Marie's power class killed me!

"Khalli, you need to move a little to loosen up. We're heading to the rink for your lesson with Jessica in a few hours," Mom encourages.

"*I knooow.* I just hurt so badly."

"But just think how strong you're going to be by the end of the summer."

"*I know.* And think what the process of getting stronger is going to *feel* like."

"You know, Khalli, no one is making you do this. You don't have to push yourself this hard."

"I'm making me do this, Mom. I have goals, and I want to achieve them. And I also want to complain along the way."

Mom grins. "Well, Khalli, it's your own choice, and your muscle pain is your own doing. So I don't want to hear it. But I do admire your work ethic."

There goes my plan to guilt-trip my mom about my pain. She's clearly not interested. One more try. "Can you make me a sandwich, Mom? Just today? Walking to the fridge is really going to hurt."

Mom laughs at me. "Not going to work, Khalli. But while you're in the kitchen, you can make me a sandwich as a thank you for taking you to the rink every day all summer."

Ugh! I push my aching body off the couch and mechanically talk my legs into taking one painful step after another to the kitchen to make not one, but two sandwiches. This is what happens when I complain.

*****

"Hey, Khalli, how are you feeling today? Because I'm a bit sore." Coach Jessica greets me with a bold smile. "I've thoroughly missed Marie's power sessions though!"

She's *missed* them? I think there's definitely something wrong with Coach Jessica. "Seriously?" I ask.

"Oh, absolutely! Marie knows how to push me to my limits. She gets me to accomplish more than I ever even imagined was possible. I've reached the level I have as a skater because she believed in me and taught me to believe in myself."

I nod, not really knowing what to say. She's right; Coach Marie has always believed I could meet her expectations, and because she's never wavered or cut me any slack, I have. Maybe it's time for me to embrace these power sessions.

"Okay, Khalli." Coach Jessica pulls me out of my thoughts. "Today we are working on your Skating Skills test patterns, and then Marie asked that we do a couple Axel drills. Is your body up for that?"

"I'll give it my best." And I really do, pushing through my muscle pain the entire lesson and practice session. Today is my light day. If I can't manage today, how will I handle three hours of ice and an off-ice class tomorrow?

CHAPTER 5

No Sympathy

I text Becky.

> Hey! Do you want to come over? Maybe watch a movie?

Within seconds, she replies.

> But it's soooo nice outside, let's go for a bike ride!

> I can't move. I'm broken.

My phone immediately rings; it's Becky. "Are you okay? What happened?" She sounds genuinely concerned.

"Power class."

"I don't even know what that means. Did you get hurt?"

"My entire life just hurts." I explain to Becky how Coach Marie pushed us to our furthest limits, and how I need to learn to appreciate this pain because I'm going to have a lot more of it this summer.

"That doesn't sound fun at all. But because you're my best friend, we can watch a movie and chill today. But next time, you know what you're walking into, so no sympathy from me if your body hurts the next day."

"Wow, I can't get sympathy from anyone, can I?"

Becky laughs and hangs up the phone. I start counting down from one hundred; she'll be here before I hit zero.

Thirty-seven, thirty-six, thirty-five, footsteps! "Hi, Auntie Krista!" Becky yells as she runs up the stairs to my room.

"I wish I could run like that!" I joke dryly as she bursts into my bedroom.

"It's overrated. Achieving your dreams is more important."

I can't help but love how much everyone has my back and is pushing me to be better. I haven't had anyone just let me sulk, and as much as I would like to, I know they are right. If I want to get better, I need to put in the work.

Becky plops down on the back of my full-size bed, tossing her backpack in between us.

"Oh! What movies did you bring?" I ask excitedly.

"I didn't. I brought beads and string to make friendship bracelets. And you're going to help me! I want to make five bracelets: one for you, Dacia, Keeloni, Tanja, and me. Next year we'll all be at different schools, so this way we'll remember to think about each other while we're apart."

"I can't imagine we'll forget!" I laugh. "But I'd love a cute bracelet!"

"Good, I'll make yours. I mean, you can't make your own friendship bracelet—that's weird. So...what do you think about these taco and unicorn beads I just got? I can string them together with some solid color beads in between."

"I think I'm going to have the most unique, and possibly ugliest, bracelet ever," I attempt to say as seriously as possible.

Becky pouts, pushing her lower lip out. "Fine, then I guess I'll use the ice skate charm that I just bought for you instead."

"Thank God!" I smile. My best friend knows exactly how to make me happy!

CHAPTER 6

A Moment with Mila

It's Thursday, which means no lessons for me. I have two hours of practice ice, followed by an hour of off-ice ballet and flexibility training, and then another hour of ice.

My coaches helped me develop a plan to better use my practice time. First I warm up with my Skating Skills patterns and work on them for the first half hour. I've been working so hard on them that Coach Marie thinks I'll be ready to test already at the end of summer! Then I work on my free skate for the next hour (jumps first and then spins until I'm dizzy), and then my program. I don't get dizzy much anymore, so I can usually do spin after spin after spin! I'm working on camel spins, the camel-sit combination, and front sit-back sit spins. Soon my coaches want me to combine them and do a camel-sit-back sit! That's one of my goals for the summer!

After off-ice, I skate some more. I'm supposed to run my program again, work on any skills I missed, and then go back to my skills patterns to cool down. Having a plan makes me so much more productive.

Coach Jessica is teaching our off-ice class. She's taking dance and choreography classes in college, so Coach Marie is having her help all her students with ballet, flexibility, and body movement.

We start with a warm-up; not everyone skated before the off-ice class started, so we need to make sure everyone is warm. Coach Jessica puts us in two staggered lines so that everyone can see her and, even more importantly, she can see everyone to make corrections.

She puts me directly between Yana and Mila. This could get awkward.

I notice Mila constantly looking over me to watch Yana. I expect to catch Yana doing the same, but I don't. Not even once. Yana is fully focused on learning from Jessica; it's like she doesn't even care that her biggest rival is six feet away from her, watching her every move.

"And stretch…" Coach Jessica draws her words out as we follow her body movements. "Look with your entire head. Your head should follow your arm through these movements."

I watch as my coach looks upward as her arm lifts toward the ceiling during our rond de jambe ballet exercise. Her movements flow with so much beauty and emotion; this is why she's so stunning on the ice! This is what I need to learn to perfect!

I glance at myself in the mirror and intently try to mimic Coach Jessica's movements. I have a lot of work to do. I shift my gaze to Yana's reflection. Her eyes bounce between my coach and her own reflection, pure focus. Next I direct my eyes toward Mila in the mirror as she watches Yana. I notice her only watching Yana, she is emulating Yana's movements, not Jessica's; it's like she's indifferent to having such a talented instructor. Her icy blue gaze settles on me and I jet my eyes back to my own reflection, but not before I catch a glimpse of her confident smirk.

After class, Mila jogs up to me. "Don't feel bad about watching me," she says full of friendliness. "It's always good to watch those who are better than you to learn." Once again, a smirk spreads across her blossom-petal pink lips.

"Oh," I reply as innocently as possible. "Is that why you were watching Yana?"

"And here I thought you were going to be cool. Guess not." Mila scoffs and sprints away.

"You are *so* cool. That was actually amazing!" Stacy comes up behind me, clearly having overheard our discussion. "But I'd stay out of this. Whatever issue Mila has with Yana isn't your problem, or mine, or even Yana's. That's for Mila to deal with. And be careful, Coach Marie doesn't take well to skaters picking fights."

I swallow hard and thank Stacy for looking out for me. I just hate how this new girl came and changed the atmosphere at my rink.

Mila is on the ice already by the time I get my skates on. She really is an amazing skater. Her jumps are gorgeous, just like Yana's. Even though I see her watching Yana regularly, Mila never slows down or takes a break. She pushes through the entire session and then stays on for the next one after I get off the ice. The girl is definitely determined, I'll give her that!

CHAPTER 7

Feet

"I want to start with your Axel today."

It's safe to say I'm in for an aggressive lesson with Coach Marie today. I've already had an hour to practice, so she knows I'm plenty warm and ready.

"Let's start with a couple back spins, and then I want to see your Axel walk-through."

The back spin, an upright spin on my right foot, represents the air position that I'll use in the Axel. Since I like to crunch up like a cannonball, Coach Marie frequently makes me review this before attempting the jump.

"Good, Khalli. Show me your walk-through. Keep your right shoulder checked back. I don't want to see your upper body rotating before you even leave the ice."

I nod.

After three very well-done walk-throughs, my coach seems satisfied.

"You've been working on these a lot on your own, haven't you?"

I grin. My hard work is evident!

We move on to the full Axel. This jump fills me with anxiety. I know I need to fully go for it if I ever want to land it, but it's the scariest thing in the world launching yourself into the air to attempt a jump that you know you don't know how to land. The other skaters have told me I will fall hundreds of times before I even get close to landing one. But if I don't give it my all and jump beyond the fear, I'll never land it. I think this is why the Axel is such a benchmark jump in skating. It's the first jump that takes genuine work and repetition to achieve. I'm not sure I've ever wanted anything more than to land this jump.

After about five attempts (three falls and two bailouts), my coach has me do a few more walk-throughs. Then back to the full jump again.

"Khalli, you have to commit," Coach Marie tells me sternly after I bail out of three jumps in a row.

"I know. I'm not trying to bail. I just can't seem to make my body do it."

"You can, and you will. You need to remember, Khalli, your mind controls your body. You have to decide to do this. You have to commit to staying in the jump. Stay over your right side, and never bail!"

I know my coach is right; she usually is. But it's not as easy as she makes it sound.

"I'll try." I promise.

We do another couple of rounds of Axels and walk-through exercises, and then my coach decides it's time to move on.

"Can I start working on these on my own? Like, the full jump, not just the walk-through?" I ask.

"You are in a safe position now, so I don't see a problem with that. Just do a handful at a time. I know how you work Khalli, and I don't want to see you doing Axels in the corner for an entire two hour session, okay?" She half-laughs as she says this because she knows that even though two hours of Axels sound like a ridiculous plan, it's kind of my style.

I agree and we move on to my spins.

*****

"Khalli, hurry up!" Becky calls anxiously up the stairs as she waits in the kitchen with my mom.

My mom is driving us to Tanja's house where we will meet up with Dacia and Keeloni. Tanja's family just got a new trampoline, and it is time for an all-girls party!

"Don't forget the Chex mix!" I yell as I run down the stairs only to see my mom already holding the covered bowl fully ready for me. "Oops! I guess you two are all ready and just waiting on me."

Becky cocks her head to the side and gives me one of her looks. "Obviously," she jokes sarcastically. "What took so long?"

"I had to wash my feet. They were in my skates all morning, and I didn't think you'd want to smell them on the trampoline all afternoon!"

"Okay, never mind! Worth the wait! And…ew!" Becky giggles.

"You're telling me! The rink was really warm today. I've never had that much foot sweat before! Apparently it's a thing in summer, the warm rink I mean. But I guess the sweaty feet too."

"Okay, stop! Gross! End of discussion!" Becky cuts me off.

"What? I'm just giving you insight into my day," I say as sweetly as possible.

"I'm glad you have good hygiene. Now can we *please* go?" Becky turns to walk out the door with the twelve-pack soda she's bringing to share. We are going to get super hyper today!

CHAPTER 8

Role Model

I kick my covers off to the incessant beeping of my alarm clock. It's 9:00 a.m., a pretty late morning for summer. The weight of my blankets is excessive! I struggle to get my exhausted legs to the ground. Why am I so tired today?

"Good morning to my loveliest daughter!" Mom smiles.

"I'm your only daughter. And I feel anything but lovely today!"

"Well, you did ask to stay up late for your girls' party, and then you were so caffeinated I'm guessing you didn't sleep right away after you went to bed. So I don't want to hear it. But I would love to hear about your ballet class and your trampoline time!"

Duh! That's why! Not only did I skate three hours and do an hour of ballet, but I also jumped up and down on a trampoline until my legs fully stopped working! I slept so deeply that yesterday seems like ages ago in my mind.

"Ballet was great! I can't get over how graceful Jessica is! She told me she wasn't born that way but kept pushing herself. I want to do the same! And there's this new girl in our class, Mila. Yana is her archenemy, but it's only on Mila's side. Yana doesn't even seem to care that Mila is there, or that she's training with Coach Marie."

Mom raises her eyebrow.

"Mila is kind of mean. I tried to welcome her, but she told me she doesn't want friends. She just wants to be better than Yana."

Mom nods, showing she's listening.

"Anyway, Mila told me she'd be nice to me since I'm a much lower-level skater and will never catch her."

Mom opens her mouth to say something, but I continue without a pause so she can't get a word in.

"I don't think she knows how quickly I've improved. I wonder what she'll say when she learns I could pass her up someday. But I don't think I care. I definitely don't want to be like her. I want to be like Yana. Yana's so busy working on her goals she doesn't even care that Mila's there, or that Mila's biggest goal is to pass her. It's crazy impressive to watch her focus, Mom. I can't even describe it. It just makes Yana even cooler."

"Well, it sounds like my loveliest daughter has chosen the right path. You always make me so proud, Khalli." Mom leans over to hug me.

"You really do know that I'm your only daughter, right?" I laugh. But I have so much to tell Mom that she doesn't even get to respond before I continue. I've been so busy I feel like I haven't seen her in days.

"And then the trampoline!" I nearly shout. "Mom! I can do my Axel on Tanja's trampoline. Tanja's little sister, Tylisa, came out to watch us, and she now wants to be a figure skater too! Because of me! How great is that?"

Mom smiles proudly but, once again, doesn't have a chance to speak because I keep talking.

"So anyway, Tanja and I want to take Tylisa skating sometime. Tanja's only gone skating once before, so she wants me to teach her little sister. Her mom said she could take us this Saturday. I know it's my day off, but can I go? Public skate is at 11:00 a.m."

"It sounds like you've already organized this," Mom says questioningly with her right eyebrow raised.

"Everything except for the asking-my-parents part." I smile innocently. "So?"

"Well, your dad and I have some things to do around the house, so I suppose we can do them while you're gone." Mom agrees to my plan. "As long as you think your body can handle skating six days next week."

"It can!" I cannot wait to teach Tanja and Tylisa.

Mom glances at the clock as she sits down with me to eat a late breakfast. We have about an hour before we have to leave for the rink. That's plenty of time to eat and get ready.

CHAPTER 9

Almost!

Fridays are my short days at the rink. I have thirty minutes to practice, thirty minutes with Coach Marie, and then another thirty minutes to practice. Compared to some of my other days where Mom drops me off and picks me up almost four or five hours later, Fridays are quick.

Coach Marie asked me to warm-up all my jumps and spins today before my lessons so that I'm completely ready for her. A half hour is enough time to warm-up with a couple of my test patterns and then still work through my free skate so I'm ready for her.

I'm set up on a hockey line, about five minutes into working on my Axel, when my coach approaches.

"Keep your right side back," she calls out as she skates toward me.

I adjust and go for another jump right away.

"Way better! Khalli, that was the best one I've seen from you!"

Coach Marie high fives me after I scrape myself up from the ice.

"I want to try again. I had a couple where I landed on my right foot before falling. I'd like you to see one so you can tell me why I'm falling. I feel my foot, and then *boom*, I'm on the ice."

Coach Marie nods, and I set up another jump.

"You jumped around yourself again. You need to jump up and out."

Coach Marie picks an advertisement banner lining the rink. "Greenery Landscaping. See the sign?"

I nod.

"If you're lining your body up on the line like you are, I want your right knee and toe to climb at the Greenery Landscaping sign."

That's right. We've talked about this before. I was definitely jumping around instead of up and out.

I try again.

And again.

Coach Marie continues to give me corrections and point out things I'm doing correctly.

"There it is!" my coach nearly shouts as I hit my right foot, slip backward off my blade, and land butt-first onto the ice.

"That's what I was doing before!" I shriek excitedly. "I feel so close! Why didn't it work?"

"Remember before how you were bailing on your jump?" She waits to see me acknowledge her. "Now you're not checking out. You're waiting until your landing foot is on the ice before you punch out of the jump, and then it's too late.

And your foot is still flexed when you're hitting the ice, so you're running out of blade. Land on your toe pick, and then absorb the landing, bending through your ankles, your knees, and then your hips. If you keep going with these corrections, you'll have it very soon! This is very huge and quick progress, Khalli!"

"How do I know exactly when to check out?" I ask.

"That's the hard part. You have to learn, more so, your body has to learn. Falling in a new jump is your body's way of figuring out what works. It's your body's learning process. Every single time you fall, you're not failing. You're teaching your body to understand what works and what doesn't. And you are doing a fantastic job of that, Khalli!"

We do several more Axels—or Axel attempts, I should say—and then we work on spins. Coach Marie gets me started on the back camel. "You're here so much this summer. I want you to have a collection of skills to work on so that you continue making progress and don't get bored."

"I could never get bored with skating!" I grin.

*****

After my ice session, I sit down next to Yana and Stacy to take my skates off. They are busy talking about Stacy's new spin combo; it's so beautiful.

"Hey, Khalli! Your Axel is really close! I'm impressed at how quickly it's coming along!" Stacy smiles.

I thank her just as Mila sits down across from me. "Yeah, how long have you been working on that?" Mila asks, her voice laced with sarcasm.

"I started Monday." I smile.

Mila looks to Stacy to confirm, and Stacy nods. "Khalli is intense, one of the hardest workers here."

"Well, don't get any ideas about passing me up. That will never happen," Mila says dryly as she picks up her things and moves to a bench across the room.

I look down at my feet, not sure what to say.

"Don't sweat it. She's so busy trying to prove she's the best that she doesn't have any energy left to actually become the best. You do you, Khalli. Don't waste your time with her drama. And who knows, maybe she'll come around eventually." Yana confidently stands up and heads to the pro shop for a skate sharpening.

"Yana's mindset is working for her, that's for sure. I'm buying into it more and more. You'd never guess I'm a year older than her, as mature as she is!" Stacy giggles.

CHAPTER 10

Coach Khalli

It's 10:30 a.m. on Saturday morning, and Tanja should be here soon with her mom and sister. I've picked out clothes that look as much like coaching attire as possible: black leggings, leg warmers, and a red fleece sweatshirt with a black vest. I grab a cream-colored hat and the thickest pair of mittens I have. I've learned very quickly that ice rinks are cold if you're not skating with your full energy; this is why coaches are always bundled. I don't think I'll be skating too hard if I'm teaching Tanja and Tylisa.

I'm wearing my leggings but jam the rest of my gear into my skate bag. And when I say jam, I mean it! Now I know why most of the coaches have large bags or carry two! My coaching attire is thick and heavy! I'd wear it to the rink, but this Wisconsin summer is super hot and humid. That many layers is a whole lot of nope!

"They're here!" Mom calls up the steps to me.

I quickly finish pulling my skate bag zipper closed while squishing the sides together; this reminds me of the movies where people sit on their suitcase to close it. What a struggle!

Bolting down the steps and around the corner with my bag on my back, I nearly knock my mom and Mrs. Jennings over.

"Whoa, calm down!" Mom steps back, gesturing with her hands in the doorway.

Tanja's mom smiles. "Your daughter is so full of energy! I've yet to see her stop moving. I swear she jumped three hours straight on our trampoline!"

"I heard, and then I also heard her excessive complaints when it hurt her to walk the next day," Mom jokes dryly.

Mrs. Jennings laughs. "I'm excited she's going to apply her energy to teach my girls today! I haven't seen Tylisa this excited about doing a sport ever, and we've tried so many sports. I hope this clicks with her and she wants to do more!"

"Khalli definitely fell in love with skating after one try!"

"Well, Tylisa really looks up to Khalli." She turns to me, smiling. "Tylisa couldn't stop talking about you and your amazing jumps on the trampoline."

I can't help but grin back. Tanja's mom has an absolutely gorgeous smile! Perfectly straight white teeth that shine boldly against her ebony skin. This is where Tanja gets her amazing smile from: her mom!

"If she likes it, I'm happy to help you figure out how skating works, from starting in a class to eventually taking private lessons," Mom offers.

Mrs. Jennings thanks her, and I head outside to put my massive skate bag in the trunk. Climbing into the back seat,

I squeeze excitedly between Tanja and Tylisa, while Mom and Mrs. Jennings finalize details for when I'll be back.

*****

I help Tylisa put her rental skates on first and then tie my own. She's only seven, so she definitely needs some help. Tanja brought her own skates, but they were too small; so she ended up renting a pair as well. The rental skates are made of plastic instead of leather like mine. The pair Tanja got is pretty beat up; it must be a popular size.

"All right! Let's do this!" I cannot wait to teach my friend and her sister how to skate! I skip to the ice and hop on only to turn around and see them both slowly hobbling unsteadily on their blades across the rubber floor a solid twenty feet behind me.

"Just walk normally, heel to toe," I call as I see Tylisa marching across the floor toward me very unstable. Tanja grabs her sister's hand as she wobbles to try to hold her up, but Tylisa's momentum toward the ground is so much stronger than Tanja's balance. I can't help but laugh as they both plop down on the rubber matting.

Tanja untangles her legs from her little sister's, and I jump off the ice to help them both up. Teaching them to skate might be a bigger challenge than I originally thought.

We finally make it to the ice, and Tanja steps on confidently. *Boom!*

"I think these skates are a little different than mine." She laughs as she gets up.

Tylisa stares at her big sister nervously.

"C'mon, Ty! I'll help you!" Tanja smiles.

"No way! I saw you fall!" Tylisa replies half-nervously and half-jokingly. "But will *you* help me?" she asks looking at me, her big golden-brown eyes full of hope.

"That's why I'm here!" I reach for her hand and help her step cautiously onto the ice. As soon as she has both feet on the ice, she stiffens up. I feel her weight go backward as her feet start to slide out in front of her. "I've got you!" I gasp as I wrap my arms around her to hold her up.

"Stand tall," I instruct. "Keep your shoulders over your feet. Bend your knees and ankles. Now breathe." I tell her as I realize she's holding her breath. "You can do this."

Tylisa gradually relaxes and sinks her weight over her feet. I'm just glad she's tiny; I wouldn't have been able to hold her up if she were my size!

Tanja listens to the direction I give her sister and follows along. In no time, Tanja figures out how to use her rental skates and skates off to do laps around the rink. I stay with Tylisa, working to keep her on her feet. Once it looks like she can stand, we practice falling and getting up, just like I learned the first time I skated.

Judging by how hard standing was for her, we probably should have started with falling and getting up before even stepping on the ice. I guess I'll learn these things as I coach more someday.

CHAPTER 11

Sunday No-Fun Day

"Good morning, Princess!" Dad gently shakes me awake. "Are you ready for breakfast?"

I rub my groggy eyes and glance at the clock. I slept in again. Am I late for the rink?

I bolt out of bed and then realize I completely ignored my dad. "Good morning!" I smile back as I rush to grab my skating clothes.

"Khalli, it's Sunday," Dad says, his forehead wrinkled. "Are you supposed to skate today? Did I miss something?"

"Sunday? That's actually amazing because my body is pretty stiff today," I say as if I weren't confused.

"Breakfast is on the table. Mom and I made waffles and bacon, and we cut up a fresh pineapple. We have about an hour before we have to leave for church, so you have plenty of time. But I did love your morning hustle!" Dad jokes.

I shuffle sluggishly down the stairs, still in my pyjamas with Dad in tow.

"I said you had an hour, not years," Dad jokes at my slow pace.

"I'm just stiff today. I don't even know why. I didn't even skate for myself yesterday, and Friday was a light day."

"Old age," Dad replies with a wink.

"Very funny."

I pull out my chair and plop my *old* self into my seat. Mom passes me the waffles and a new bottle of real maple syrup that one of our neighbors made; this stuff is the best! Next I reach for the bacon, dropping three slices onto my plate and one onto the floor. Fail! I bend over to pick it up, but my lower back is so stiff I can't even reach the floor! Er. I grunt as I try to bounce my body lower to reach. *Er, err.*

"Khalli." Dad bends down across the table and looks at me from below the tabletop. "Is there a problem?"

"Yeah," I grunt. "I don't have a dog. And I need a dog to clean up this bacon because my back won't let me reach it."

Dad cocks his head to the side. "That's a unique argument for a dog. I don't think it's going to work on your mom, but I'm sold."

Mom shoots Dad a look as I finally manage to grasp the bacon off the floor. I inspect the bacon and take a bite out of it.

"Ew." Mom judges my decision to still eat it.

"Don't worry, I don't really need a dog." I smile, knowing we don't have enough time for a pet. "But since I don't have a dog to fully clean up my mess, could you maybe wipe up the bacon grease on the floor? I can't reach it."

Mom hands me a spray bottle and towel. I guess that's a no. What a bad day to drop my bacon! Why am I so sore anyway?

*****

In the car on the way to church, I felt every bump in the road. At church, the pews had never felt so stiff. I helped take the offering, and man, that offering plate was heavy! The ride home felt even bumpier, and then Mom and Dad announced that today was family yard workday.

"I thought Sundays were family days. You know, Sunday Fun Day."

"It is a family day, and together, we are going to make our yard beautiful," Dad says as if it's going to be fun.

Mom and Dad explain how we are planting a new tree in the front yard, and they want to frame it in fieldstones and dump red mulch around the tree. "Grandpa has a young birch tree he wants to get rid of, so he's delivering it later today. We need to be ready. But don't worry, Khalli, your mom and I will dig the hole. Your job is simply to move the extra fieldstones from a pile in the back of the house into the front yard while we dig. Nothing too difficult."

I don't think my parents understand how sore my back is today. But I know I need to help out at home if I want to continue to skate, so there's no point in arguing.

I slowly make my way to the backyard to pick up the fieldstones and move them one by one. I squat down and wrap my arms around a large purplish granite rock and lift it up as pain warms my lower back. Man, this rock might be as heavy as Tylisa.

Oh, duh. Obviously.

My back hurts because I was holding up Tylisa. I think I might need to work on my coaching skills a bit still so I'm not so sore next time. So much for my relaxing weekend off!

I carry my rock to the front and drop it where Mom and Dad's tools are laying and return to get another. I make eight trips with eight large rocks before my parents come back outside.

"Wow! Khalli! Have you been carrying these one by one? You really are serious about your training. If you get tired, you can always use the wheelbarrow. I set it by the garage door for you. Maybe just push a few rocks at a time so it's not too heavy."

Is he serious? I could have used the wheelbarrow for all these? But instead here I am carrying rocks the size of a second-grader around! Part of me wants to scream, but the other part of me is so thankful to have a wheelbarrow. I sulk across the front yard to get the wheelbarrow and spend the next hour pushing rocks around. *This is training. This is training,* I repeat in my head over and over. If today doesn't kill me, I should be able to handle any power class Coach Marie throws at me this summer!

CHAPTER 12

Not Cut Out to Be a Figure Skater

I always look forward to my lessons with Coach Marie, but today I feel differently. Skating hurts. In fact, walking hurts, standing hurts, sitting hurts—everything hurts! I'm not sure how much of the pain from my throbbing muscles is coming from Saturday with Tylisa and how much is coming from Sunday Fun Day—if I can even call it that.

I tell Coach Marie right away about my aches at the beginning of my lesson. I'm not looking for excuses. I just want her to be aware that I'm hurting, and I also want to brag a little about my first coaching experience.

"That's so great that you helped your friend's little sister skate! But you need to be careful, Khalli. You're not a full-size adult. I'll bet the little girl was half your size."

"Oh, at least!"

"When we coach younger skaters, we usually start by teaching them how to fall and get up first, and we often do this on the ground before getting on the ice. Next we teach them how to stand, then you don't need to hold them up as much."

"That would have been good to know! I figured out that I missed the falling and getting up lesson a bit too late."

"It's a ton of work trying to hold a skater up. If you decide you want to help your friend again, let me know, and I'll give you some tips to keep you from breaking your back and to help her understand how to stand and then skate."

"I would really like that." I smile. "Let me check with Tylisa and see if she wants to come again. I think she had fun."

"Okay. And, Khalli." Coach Marie pauses. "I really think it's wonderful that you want to share your passion with your friends and their siblings. I just want to help ensure that neither of you get hurt and that it's fun for everyone."

I nod. Maybe I should have watched a beginner class before jumping out on the ice to coach.

"Let's start with your Skating Skills today. That will be a little less aggressive than free skate. I'd like to see your forward crossovers on a circle. We are really going to focus on using your under push today."

Normally I prefer free skate lessons; however, today I'm grateful that I don't need to throw my body into the air—a fall might be the end of me! Skating Skills sound like the perfect way to still make progress despite how sore I am.

"Fix your fingers!" Coach Marie picks on my wide-stretched fingers; spider fingers, as some of the other skaters at Berger Lake Ice Center say. I pull my fingers closer together and soften my hand. It's always good when Coach Marie starts picking on my fingers; it means she's running out of other things to adjust! I fight to point my toe and turn it out, bending into my ankles as much as I possibly can. I can feel my blade driving into the ice as I push. I'm gaining so much power, and I absolutely love it! If I think about my movements enough, I can almost think past my aches and pains.

"Okay, other direction!" my coach yells after a couple of other corrections. Clockwise is so much harder for me; it just doesn't feel natural.

"Stroke your foot across the ice when you cross it! I want crossovers, not step overs!"

We've talked about this so many times. I know this. But why is it so hard? I fight to make my left foot graze the ice as I stroke through my crossover.

"Bend into your ankles more. Point your left toe inward as you cross!" Coach Marie calls out instructions as I focus to make adjustments. "Better! Now push! Let's go! Push, cross, push, cross!" She's nearly shouting, chasing me around the circle. "Follow my tempo! Push! Cross! Push! Every stroke is a push! Use it!"

Oh my God. I don't know how much longer I can do this! My heart is pounding.

"Three more laps. Let's go, Khalli! Push! Cross! Push!"

I count down to my last lap, hopeful I can make it.

"Good, Khalli! Why don't you grab a drink of water and then we'll do the same thing for your backward crossovers."

So much for taking today easy!

We spend the rest of our lesson working, and I mean it when I say *working*, through my skills. If I push myself hard enough, I think I can have my next test ready before summer is over. And if I can make it through today's pain, I should be able to handle anything!

After setting my water bottle down, I pause and take a big breath. Today I really need to push myself to keep going.

"Taking a break, I see. Not everyone was cut out to be a figure skater."

I don't even need to look to know who it is: Mila.

"At least I was on time for my ice session." I smirk as I skate back to my coach.

"My dad was late," she mutters, slamming her guards down.

"What was that all about?" my coach asks, her hazel eyes fiercely piercing through me.

Shoot! My face must have given away my encounter with Mila. Coach Marie saw it.

I don't respond. What can I even say? I look over my shoulder and see Mila storming off into the lobby. Maybe it was more than just my face that gave it away.

"Mila and I don't get along," I finally say.

Coach Marie nods slowly but doesn't say anything.

"I don't like that she hates Yana, so I stood up for Yana. And now she hates me. What's her deal with Yana anyway?"

"Maybe this will help you understand," Coach Marie begins. "Who beat you at the last competition?"

"Nellie Blancherd. But I don't get how it matters. I plan to beat her next time anyway."

"The way you remember her name and feel competitive toward Nellie…well, Mila and Yana feel the same. These two have been competing against each other consistently for three years. Mila usually takes a close second to Yana, and on occasion, Yana is second to Mila. Yana just moved up a level, and Mila wants to catch her. I will not discourage healthy competition. It makes both skaters work harder and achieve more. But I do disagree with poor sportsmanship, so my eyes are very open, Khalli. I'm watching both girls like a hawk to make sure things don't intensify. I'm also watching my other students to make sure they don't get in the middle of it."

I swallow. That comment was clearly about me.

"Mila said you're a better coach than her last coach. Are you?" I ask.

"Mila trained with Marko Jameson. He's a fantastic coach, but it sounds like things weren't working out due to some recent events, which is why she needed a change."

"It sounds like she can't work things out with anyone." I snuff.

Coach Marie gives me a disapproving look.

"Understand this, Khalli. My skaters *will* get along. You don't need to be best friends, but I expect respect from each and every one of you toward each other."

I sink my head ashamed. "But what about Yana? How does she feel about you coaching her competition?"

"Not that it's the business of everyone at the rink, but to help you understand the drive that leads to success, I'm going to tell you. I talked with Yana before accepting Mila as a student. Yana has been my student for several years, so I have a responsibility to look out for her before accepting a new student who may create an issue for Yana. Do you know what Yana said?"

I shake my head.

"She told me to bring it on! She asked me to coach Mila so that she would have more pressure to improve and not to slack. Her goal has nothing to do with Mila. She wants to be the absolute best she can be. Yana actually said having Mila here gives her a chance to gauge her progress by working to stay a level above Mila. She wants to keep Mila in her rear-view mirror as she drives straight into her success and dreams. Yana is fierce, so fierce, that she welcomes the competition."

Wow. I don't even know what to say. I don't think I would feel the same if Coach Marie started training my competitors. I admire Yana even more now.

"That being said, Mila is having a really hard time being here. She realizes now that she came across a bit aggressive her first week."

"A bit? Even today she just told me I wasn't cut out for figure skating or something like that."

Coach Marie gives me a sad smile. "Her first impression has been rough. I get it. This has been a hard transition for her as well. I don't know what she wants people to know, but just know that she's struggling, and switching from Marko Jameson was about more than she's telling you."

"I just wish she was nicer. I tried to be her friend," I say quietly.

"Maybe you should try again," my coach encourages. "Now back to these crossovers! I want to see full underpushes. Let's go!"

CHAPTER 13

Emergency!

It's Tuesday, and that means power class. Ugh! I'm so glad I'm not as sore today as I was yesterday. This is going to be brutal! I'm grabbing one last drink of water in preparation for what's to come as Mila steps onto the ice. "I see you're taking a break again."

I'm ready to fire back at her when Coach Marie's words from yesterday hit me. I decide to do the right thing. Taking a deep breath, I turn to Mila.

"I'm sorry for picking on you for being late yesterday. It's not your fault your dad was behind schedule."

Mila rolls her eyes. "He's always late now ever since we moved out."

I don't even know what to say; that wasn't the answer I was expecting.

"I'm sorry. That must be rough."

"That's not even the half of it. You have no idea," Mila bluntly responds before skating off to class.

Well, I suppose that went better than any other conversation we've had. At least her anger wasn't directed at me.

I push my way through power class. I swear Coach Marie enjoys causing us misery! Coach Jessica seems to enjoy the struggle, as do Yana and Mila. I apparently need to get stronger if this is so exhausting for me!

I have an hour to practice after power class. My Jell-O legs make it really difficult, but if I ever want to land this Axel, I need to dedicate some serious time to practicing it.

*****

Emergency! Come to my house!
Like now!

I read Becky's message on my phone when I step off the ice. I look at the time: Becky sent this forty-five minutes ago. Shoot!

My fingers fumble as I struggle to text as quickly as possible.

What happened? Is everything okay?

No response.
I call. Voicemail. Now I'm worried.
I text Auntie Liz.

Is Becky okay?

I imagine so. She's at home with Rudy.
Should I be worried?

I don't want to worry Auntie Liz, but Becky said it's an emergency. Just as I'm about to hit Send on a long message to Auntie Liz explaining what I know, I get a message from Becky.

> I'm fine. But I need your help! ASAP!
> And don't tell my mom—I believe they are
> conspiring!!

I no longer have any clue what we're talking about, but I assume it's Becky being Becky again—and that means weirdness! I delete my message to Auntie Liz and type, "All is well, don't worry," and then tell Becky I can be there in thirty minutes.

Auntie Liz types back immediately.

> When someone tells a mom don't
> worry, she worries! ;)

I respond with laughing emojis and hurry to take my skates off. I am now on a schedule. I grab my bags and rush through the lobby.

"Bye, Khalli," Mila says softly as I walk past her.

I'm completely caught off-guard but do my best to pretend I'm not. "Have a good day, Mila." I smile. I see Stacy's eyes bulge in overhearing our words. I kind of wish I wouldn't have played it so tough against Mila in the beginning.

CHAPTER 14

Mission Accepted

As soon as I get home, I peel myself out of my sweaty skating clothes and rush to rinse off in the shower. I have no idea what's so urgent, but the faster I hurry, the sooner I'll know. I throw on jean shorts and an airy tank top as my phone dings. It's Becky.

Wear all-black.

Seriously, I was just wearing all-black for the entire morning at the rink.

At least with being a figure skater, I have an entire drawer full of black clothing. I grab a pair of black gym shorts and a black fitted tank; it's way too hot out to wear my thick skating leggings. I tie a black zip-up around my waist just in case I actually need more black. What is Becky getting me into today?

"Gotta go, Mom. Becky needs me!"

"Have fun! Stay out of trouble!" Mom jokes on my way out the door.

I bolt down the sidewalk and dash up Becky's porch steps, straight through the front door, around the corner, and up the stairway directly into her bedroom, body-slamming into her older brother, Rudy.

"Where's Becky?"

"Hey, Khalli! So great to see you too! How are you doing?" Rudy asks half-jokingly and half-seriously.

"I'm good. Sorry! Becky said it was an emergency, so I rushed over here and—sorry, how are you?"

"I'm doing very well," Rudy says with a semi-twisted smile. "I see she's pulling you into it, huh?"

"Into what?" *I'm so confused.*

"If so, you'll know soon enough," Rudy hints before slinking off down the hall.

I plop down on Becky's bed and text her.

> Where are you? I'm in your room. Was expecting you here, not Rudy.

Becky replies immediately.

> What?!?!

Exactly eight seconds later, I hear Becky's footsteps pounding through the house.

"Rudy was in here? What's the damage? Where was he? Did he touch anything?" she nearly shouts.

"Um, am I supposed to know the answer to this? He was leaving your room as I ran in. What's going on?"

"We need to do a full inspection. Like right now!" Becky insists.

"Not until you tell me what's going on!" My arms are folded across my chest, and my voice comes out sounding like my mother's; that's a bit scary!

"It's war, Khalli! You've walked into a war!"

I tilt my head in confusion. It doesn't look like war.

"Rudy! He's the enemy!"

"I love you too!" Rudy calls from the hallway as he jogs past.

"What are you doing now!?" Becky bolts past me and out the door; she's clearly lost it.

Rudy pushes her back into the room and closes the bedroom door behind her, holding the doorknob so she can't escape. "Make your move, Beck! And make it well!" An evil laugh follows his words.

"I have to win!" Becky whispers to me. "You have to help me! Let's figure out what he did to my room."

As we start pulling her room apart, Becky explains how she and Rudy started a prank war and he keeps winning. So far he's put frosting in her conditioner bottle and wrapped her bar of soap in Saran Wrap so when she scrubbed, it was useless.

"And he stole my pillow and filled my pillowcase with packing peanuts! And flipped my doorknob around so he could lock it from the outside! He replaced my soccer shoelaces with pipe cleaners and dumped out my Kool-Aid and replaced it with lemon juice and food coloring. Do you know how disgusting that is?"

"Wow! He's good!"

"Don't compliment the enemy, Khalli! He also swapped out my ChapStick with a glue stick and the final kicker this morning. He gave me a hard-boiled egg to peel, *except it wasn't hard boiled*!" she practically screams. "I had egg everywhere! And I had already showered with my plastic soap and frosting conditioner. I have to get him back, and I *need* your help!"

I'm trying so hard not to giggle. These pranks are brilliant! But poor Becky!

"All right, I think we need to make a plan."

"Duh!" Becky nearly giggles despite her frustration.

"What have you done to him so far?" I ask.

"I put doorstops under the rec room door so he couldn't open it outward. I replaced his lunch meat with fabric-felt slices that looked similar. And I've hacked into his social media accounts and posted that he has the best sister in the world," she announces proudly.

"That's it? It sounds like he is winning big time," I blurt out dryly.

"Thanks. I know. This is why I need your help! Mom knows we're pranking each other and says we better not do anything that's not safe or affects our friendships, so that kind of limits me."

"Does it? Maybe you just need to think outside the box."

"Duh, again! That's why I need you, Khalli."

"Mission accepted!" I smile boldly. Dare I say, I'm even flattered!

CHAPTER 15
Preparation

I make Becky tell me about all Rudy's daily activities, habits, and anything else that might serve as a pranking opportunity.

"He gets up every morning at 5:45 a.m. and showers. Then he leaves for his summer job by 6:30 a.m. because he usually has to bike there if Mom and Dad are using both of the vehicles. He packs his lunch, checks his email, and then he's out the door."

"What does he eat for lunch?" I investigate further.

"He usually makes a sandwich. Turkey, cheese, and lettuce. No one else really eats sandwiches here, so that's why swapping out his lunch meat seemed easy. Apparently the felt-style meat didn't feel the same, so he knew before he even made his sandwich."

"Um, duh!" I laugh. "Does he use butter or mayonnaise on his sandwiches?"

"Nope. Mustard."

"Gross!"

"Right?"

"But functional…" I hint suspiciously.

"What are you thinking?"

"I'm thinking it'd be helpful to inspect his mustard."

"It's useless. It's a creamy honey mustard in a clear bottle. He'd see if we tampered with it."

"Or would he? C'mon! I need a sample of that mustard!"

"But you don't like mustard, Khalli."

"And neither will he!"

We dash off to the kitchen and sneak his mustard bottle out of the fridge. Becky's fridge is pretty packed full, so as long as we get it back before Rudy makes a sandwich, he'll never know it's missing!

I tuck the mustard bottle into the black sweatshirt that I tied around my waist. I knew this would come in handy! "Wait! Why am I wearing all-black, Becky?"

"To look the part, obviously! This is how robbers dress on TV, so we've dressed accordingly."

Seems like decent logic. I can't fault Becky's thinking one bit!

"We need to sneak to my house. I have a plan!"

Becky chases after me down the sidewalk. She doesn't ask a single question. She clearly trusts my idea without even knowing what it is. And she should: it's a good one!

"Follow my lead," I whisper outside our front door.

Trying to act normal, I open the door, and we head to the kitchen. "Hey, Mom!"

"Hey, Auntie Krista!"

Mom greets us and then goes back to whatever she was doing on her phone.

"Hey, Mom! Can you teach us how to make mashed potatoes? Becky and I were just talking about how we haven't had them forever. You know, the amazing extra creamy kind without skins."

Becky tries to play along despite clearly being clueless. "Khalli always says you make them the best!"

"Well, you girls sure know how to make a mom feel good about her mashed potatoes! I would love to pass on my secrets to the next generation. How about we make them for dinner tonight?"

"Can we make them now? I'm so hungry from being at the rink."

Mom looks at me like I'm crazy but then sets down her phone and joins us at the counter. "All right. I suppose this is a healthy enough snack. Why not?" She grabs a sack of russet potatoes and hands Becky and I each a peeler. "Go to town, ladies! When they are all peeled, I'll teach you how to boil them."

"Thanks, Mom!" I say more with more enthusiasm than she was expecting. "Trust me," I whisper to Becky.

*****

After about fifteen minutes of peeling, the potatoes are ready. We watch as Mom fills the massive pot with water, sprinkles some salt in, and sets the stovetop to boil. "This will be a while, ladies. Why don't you come back in thirty minutes."

"Seriously? You spend this much time making us dinner every night?" I ask, baffled. I clearly never paid attention to how much effort Mom put into feeding our family.

Mom smiles and shoes us away with her hand.

Becky and I skip off to my room where I fill her in on my plan. "This is brilliant, Khalli! Absolutely brilliant! He'll never know."

I smile proudly. I really hope this turns out well.

While we wait for the potatoes to cook, I have Becky fill me in on the rest of Rudy's daily activities. This is going to be tough! We get to Rudy's evening schedule, and I only have a couple basic and kind of lame ideas. "Wait, wait! Backtrack to the beginning of the day again!" I command.

Becky starts over and gets to the part about Rudy biking to work. "I got it!" I burst out excitedly.

"Mom said it's got to be safe though. This makes it complicated."

"No, it doesn't." I smile knowingly. "Now come on. Let's go finish these potatoes!"

"You're not going to tell me your other plan!?" Becky is nearly begging.

"I can't yet. I haven't fully completed my vision of the perfect prank!" I grab Becky's wrist and start to drag her out of my room.

"You don't need to pull. I'm excited enough about these potatoes to beat you there!" Becky squeals as she races past me down the stairs.

CHAPTER 16

The Mustard Factory

"All right, ladies, extra creamy potatoes coming right up! You're lucky you didn't choose the sour cream mashed baby red potatoes because I just looked in the fridge and realized I don't have sour cream."

"That's fine. I'm really craving the creamy ones!" It's not a lie; I've never wanted these mashed potatoes more in my life!

Mom teaches us how to drain boiling water from the potatoes carefully. Then she helps us measure out butter and milk into a saucepan.

"You ladies are going to stir this on low until the butter is completely melted, and then comes the fun part."

We do as Mom asks while she pulls her KitchenAid mixer forward on the counter so Becky and I can reach it.

"Melted! Next!" I shout excitedly when the last speck of butter disappears into the now pastel yellow milk.

"I never thought you'd be so excited to learn a recipe." Mom smiles, thoroughly enjoying this. "You can use the potato masher, which I'm tempted to make you do since you have so much energy. But the faster option to ultimate creamy potatoes is to dump the milk and melted butter into the mixer bowl along with the potatoes."

Mom helps us so we don't burn ourselves; the pot full of drained potatoes is heavy!

"And mix!"

Becky and I watch patiently as the KitchenAid does all the work.

"What kind of gravy would you girls like?"

Becky and I look at each other. Shoot! If we don't make gravy, Mom will know something's up.

"Actually, Auntie Krista, I really just like salt and pepper on my potatoes." Becky saves the day!

"What an easy kid! You okay with that as well, Khalli?"

I nod, not trying to look too eager.

"Let's eat them outside!" Becky squeals excitedly, seeing the creamy potatoes.

"Normally I would tell you no, but I have work to do today. So just use paper bowls and plastic silverware. Toss it when you're done."

Mom's been working part-time at a flexible new job from home to help pay for my skating. Sometimes it's frustrating that she's so busy, but today it works out.

"C'mon!" Becky grabs my hand after filling two bowls to the brim with potatoes. "The rest you can save for dinner. Thanks for teaching us how to cook!" she yells back to my mom as she pulls me through the front door. We giggle the entire way to her house. This is going to be epic!

"Now we need to sneak into my house and grab the food coloring. You wait here with the potatoes," she orders.

I sit on her front porch, eating my potatoes, while Becky scavenges through her kitchen cabinets. These really are delicious, and I was actually quite hungry. Who would have thought I would have had so much fun learning how to cook with my mom and Becky. I kind of want to do it again and learn to make something else; and next time, not just for a prank.

"Seriously, Khalli?" Becky rushes out of her door, food coloring in hand. "These are for Rudy!"

"Mm. Yep. Those are." I point to Becky's bowl while scraping the bottom of my bowl clean.

"Do I get to try any?"

"Sure do." I grab her spoon, fill it from her bowl, and raise it to her mouth. "It's an even better prank if your germaphobe brother knows you licked the spoon first!"

Becky giggles and shoves the spoon in her mouth. "These are delicious! And easy! I like it!"

"All right. Time to get to work!"

Becky sets the mustard and food coloring right between us on the porch step. "Let's color match!"

We carefully add drops of yellow food coloring to the potatoes with a splash of red until it matches the mustard perfectly. "The texture is perfect!" Becky gushes with an evil laugh.

She squeezes the mustard out into a small container so it doesn't go to waste.

"I hate the smell of mustard!" I squeeze my nose.

We stuff the mustard bottle with our mashed potato concoction and add a drop of mustard at the top so it still smells right when Rudy opens it.

"Oh my goodness! It looks identical!" Becky swoons. "I can't wait for Rudy to eat his sandwich at work tomorrow! I don't think it'll be gross, so he'll get to eat still, but it is not going to taste the way he expects! I think this is a victory!"

She practically jumps at me, giving me a massive hug. "Thank you, Khalli! I knew I could count on you!"

"Oh, we're not done with Rudy yet." I quip as we sneak into the house to put the potato-mustard in the fridge and hide the real mustard.

CHAPTER 17

Epic!

"What do you think of this?" I screech, pulling pink and purple streamers out of our craft drawer. "*Oh!* And this!" I hold up some pink sparkle ribbon.

Becky is giggling out of control and can't respond; that only encourages me to keep going.

"And this glitter yarn! We can knot it around his handlebars like a friendship bracelet. It'll take forever for him to get it off! He'll actually have to ride his bike to work looking like he stole it from his kid sister!"

Becky has lost it. She's curled into the tiniest ball on my floor, snorting away in a giggle fit.

"I-I—oh, I—"

"What, Becky? I can't understand you!" I'm laughing so intensely now that she can probably hardly understand me.

"I can't!" She gasps for air. "I-I can't even!"

Becky's arms are wrapped tightly across her stomach, and every note of laughter causes her to pull her head forward off the floor and then twitch with her legs to avoid smashing her head backward into the floor.

"My tummy hurts!" she manages to squeak.

As soon as we were done creating the mustard-wanna-be potato sauce, I let Becky into my next revenge idea: turning Rudy's bike into every five-year-old girl's dream! And of course, she loved it!

"And this!" I hold up strands of silver tinsel left over from last Christmas.

Becky's not even looking at me as she agrees through continued giggles, tears pouring out of her eyes.

"Becky! Pull yourself together and snap out of it! We're on a mission, and you're failing!"

More giggles followed by gasps for air, two big snorts, and finally a great big inhale. I hold myself together as best I can, but watching Becky fall apart into laughter is one of my favorite things in the world.

"I'm not failing," she finally manages to say. "I chose the best partner in crime, and because she's brilliant and on my team, I am also winning!"

"I can't argue with your logic…but we still have work to do."

"I know, but I haven't told you the best part of your incredible plan." Becky pauses, and I wait, making not-so-patient gestures as she gathers her words and gets her breath back.

"Rudy's new girlfriend works with him, and he bikes to her house in the morning so they can ride together to work!"

I squeal. Like, actually squeal. Within a couple of seconds, I find myself balled up on the floor, holding my stomach in a mess of giggles and snorts just like Becky two minutes ago. Becky plops down next to me, and we lose it together. This is going to be epic!

CHAPTER 18

A Mindset like Yana

Becky and I decorated late into the night. We wanted to make sure Rudy didn't have a chance to see his bike before he went to bed. Becky doesn't have a bedtime in summer, and my Wednesday lesson with Coach Jessica isn't until 11:00 a.m. today; so Mom said I could stay at Becky's until 9:30 last night! If she only knew what she allowed us to do!

I spent the morning sleeping in and woke up just in time to get ready for the rink. I grab my phone for the day as soon as I finish my late breakfast and nearly shriek at the text from Becky.

> Omg Omg O.M.G!!! Khalli—it was amazing! Ask me what Rudy did?! We're too brilliant!

> OMG What?!?! I can't wait! Tell me now!!!!

I stare at my phone for three minutes, waiting for a response—nothing. My mind drifts off into thoughts of Rudy panicking.

"Khalli! We're on a schedule!" Mom calls me out of my imagination.

Becky!!?!!?!

Still nothing. Shoot! I should have gotten up earlier. Now I probably won't know until I get off the ice.

I scramble to get ready and hop in the car, skate bag in hand. I'm going to really have to work to focus today; I can't think about anything other than Rudy probably screaming and chasing Becky around the house. We definitely won!

*****

Mom drops me off in front of the rink and drives off to do her grocery shopping. Yana is the only person in the lobby; either I'm really early, or I'm late for the start of the session.

"Hey, Khalli! Want to do some off-ice jumps with me? Ice is running ten minutes behind today. Some Zamboni issues this morning apparently."

"Absolutely!" I drop my bag and skip over to where Yana is practicing off-ice double loops. "I keep hoping the more off-ice Axels I do, the easier it will get on ice!"

"That's exactly how it works!"

68

Yana and I do jumps for almost ten minutes side by side. We don't say much; she's very focused so I don't want to interrupt. I'm dying to ask her about Mila though.

Every once in a while, she stops to catch her breath and watches my Axel. "Careful not to round your takeoff, watch your right hip when you land, and check to the right on your landing." Yana throws a couple of tips my way. I know exactly what she means when she says these things; Coach Marie has walked me through these corrections so many times, but I appreciate the reminder to think about these things when Yana mentions them.

Yana moves on to off-ice double Axels; she's so incredible to watch, and so determined. I continue with my single Axel, really focusing on the climb.

"We should get our skates on!" Yana says, jogging over to the bench where her bag is. I race after her. If I want to improve, I need to try to keep up with the best skaters at our rink, and Yana is one of them.

Lacing up my skates, I decide to ask Yana about Mila. "Does it bother you that she's so determined to beat you? It's like she thinks of nothing other than becoming better than you. Doesn't that make you angry?"

Yana doesn't even need time to think before responding. "It's not about her. My training is about me. If she's chasing me, then I don't have time to turn around and watch her. That will only hold me back. I will use Mila's chase to push me further. And to be honest, the fact that she's so obsessed with beating me…well, I'm actually flattered."

Wow. I don't even know how to respond. But I don't really have time to anyway. Yana already has both skates on and is walking toward the rink. "See you out there, Khalli!"

I scramble to lace up my second skate; how is she so fast?

A group of skaters comes into the lobby. This means their session is over, and I'm late for mine! Just as I'm jumping up to head to the ice, Mila sits down across from me.

"Hi, Mila!" I say with maximum effort.

"Hi, Khalli."

The driest response possible but hey! At least she's taken the effort to learn my name. I smile softly at her before scurrying off to my lesson with Coach Jessica.

*****

"Sorry I'm late!"

Coach Jessica nods. "Everything is off timing-wise today. So let's not worry about it. Time to warm up!"

I tell her I already warmed-up with off-ice Axels for ten minutes, and she agrees to go straight to jumps. "Just two laps around the rink first to feel your edges, and then we'll jump. Perimeter power stroking. Go!"

I race off to work my edges. *Push, cross, hold!* I think to myself as I perform crossovers followed by inside edges.

"Khalli! Those are getting so much better!" Coach Jessica applauds me. "By the time this pattern shows up on your next test, you'll already be ready for it!"

I grin. I can't wait to be on my third test. On Friday, Coach Marie is going to pick my second Skating Skills test apart, so that means today is a free skate day!

"Let's warm up your jumps! Waltz jump, go!"

I power across the ice into my waltz jump. My coaches have been working with me to increase my climb into this jump; they want a big split. I push my weight through my foot and up to my toe pick as I launch forward. Stretching my right leg in front of me, I soar forward before snapping over my right side to prepare for the landing. That felt amazing. I hope Coach Jessica liked it!

"Khalli! You must have been working on this!"

I smile; she liked it.

"That's the kind of push I want to see into your Axel! But not that much split. Not yet anyway." She winks.

We work through my other jumps before moving onto the Axel. My Axel walk-throughs are good, so Coach Jessica decides it's time to go for the full Axel.

I line up on a hockey line and push into it: one-and-a-half rotations of sheer determination. Boom! I pick myself up off the ice as Coach Jessica reminds me to keep my right side back on the takeoff. And again! Boom! I must have scraped myself off the ice two dozen times already.

"All right. Let's move on. We don't need any more bruises today. Let's spin." Coach Jessica motions to the center of the rink where she'd like me to set up my spins.

"I'd like to keep going with the Axel if that's okay. I feel so close. I'm hitting my right foot but just sliding off of it. I really think I can do this today."

"Well, who am I to hold you back!" Coach Jessica laughs. "All right, let's do some more!"

After another few minutes, I'm even closer but also thoroughly exhausted. Since she can see my muscles are becoming weak, Coach Jessica suggests we move on to spins. This time I willingly agree.

We skate off to center ice where I start with a scratch spin—what a nice break for my tired body! Falling wears me out fast!

CHAPTER 19

Played

By the time I get off the ice, my phone is plastered with notifications—all from Becky!

> Khalli! You need to call me! You need to know!
>
> Hey Khalli—hurry up and finish skating!
>
> OMG it's killing me that you don't know. Call me!

It's killing me that I don't know as well! I rush to get my skates off so I can talk to Becky.

Tossing my skate bag over my shoulder, I call Becky with the other hand.

"Oh my God, Khalli!" she practically screams. "I've been dying to tell you this! You can't even imagine. This morning was epic, and that was before Rudy sent me pictures of his sandwich: chewed-up-and-spit-out pictures of his mashed potato sandwich!"

"*Eeew*," I interrupt Becky, who has yet to take a breath.

"Yeah, you're telling me! I had to open my phone to it. I laughed so hard though. But come over, like right now!"

"How about in twenty minutes? I'm still at the rink."

Becky lets out the most massive sigh right into my ear. "I guess..."

"I'll be there as soon as I can!" I promise with enthusiasm.

Becky hangs up just as my mom pulls into the parking lot. "Let's go!" I nearly shriek as I toss my bag into the back seat.

"Okay, sure. But you need to sit down, close the door, and buckle first!" Mom laughs. "What's the hurry?"

"Becky! I need to get to Becky's." I make sure not to say more.

"Does this have anything to do with Rudy's mashed potato sandwich?" Mom jeers, looking at me out of the corner of her eye. "Hungry for mashed potatoes, huh?"

"You know?" I draw out with confusion.

"Moms know everything. Don't worry, I'll get you back."

"Get me back? But—"

"You and Becky tricked me into making mashed potatoes, so now I'm an accomplice. If I'm going to be guilty, I'm going to be guilty for something good! So just wait!"

"Uh-oh," is all I manage to squeak out. I guess Mom talked to Auntie Liz.

After a moment of pure silence, Mom finally breaks. "But it was actually brilliant! Liz and I laughed so hard. You girls got him good!"

"So you're not mad? Thank God!"

"Mad? No. Annoyed that I got played and determined to get you and Becky back, yes. But thanks for helping me maintain my innocence through Becky and Rudy's war. I wouldn't have helped if I knew what I was contributing to. So well played! But now, payback!"

Ugh! But seriously, what could my mom actually come up with to trick Becky and I?

I sprint in the house, dropping my skate bag in the mudroom. I rush up to my room to change from my rink clothes into summer apparel.

"Bye!" I shout forty-five seconds later as I bolt down the steps and toward the door.

Mom looks up from her laptop on the kitchen table as I dash past her. "Take your time. The longer you're gone, the more time I have to plan my revenge!"

Ugh! I really hope she's kidding!

I race down the street and plow through Becky's front door. "Hey, Auntie Liz!" I blurt as I scramble up the stairs to Becky's room.

"Hey, Miss Trouble!" I hear Auntie Liz's voice fading as I get to the top of the stairs.

"Tell me everything!" I blurt out as I plow into Becky's room. "And don't leave anything out!"

"Oh my God, Khalli! It's about time! I'm bursting with the details!

"So tell me!"

Becky takes a deep breath and lets it out. Just as I'm getting impatient, she frantically starts talking a mile a minute, and I struggle to even hear individual words. She's not even talking in complete sentences, just straight rambling.

"So Rudy went into the garage this morning and within seconds I heard him screaming my name, I was awake because I set my alarm, I didn't want to miss anything. I had to fight myself to stay in my bed and pretend I was sleeping as he came barreling up the stairs and straight into my room. I was giggling so hard my entire bed was shaking so he knew I wasn't sleeping."

Quick breath. And then, "Rudy ripped the covers off my bed yelling about how I destroyed his bike, apparently he thought some of the plastic wrap we used was paint and that his bike was actually a little girl's bike forever. I think that's a compliment to our quality workmanship, although when I tried to tell him this he was not the slightest bit amused. He calmed down a bit when I told him it wasn't paint but then insisted I get up to help him clean up his bike so he could leave for work on time. I pretended to fall back asleep which made him so irritated he started jumping on my bed—I felt like I was on a trampoline!

"Mom of course heard the ruckus and came rushing into my room. One glimpse at Rudy jumping on my bed and she thought he had literally gone mad so she dove in to pull him off me. He was already on the upward bounce and couldn't stop once he saw her, bounced his shoulder off of her face and her nose started gushing blood! You know how she gets bloody noses easily. But even though her bloody face is normal, Rudy panics and freezes. This of course gives me enough time to break free from my blankets and escape to the other side of the room." Deep breath.

My mouth is completely open at this point. Becky continues before I can even ask if Auntie Liz was okay. I know she was because I saw her for 0.3 seconds on my way to Becky's room, so I guess I can get more details later.

"So Rudy sees me and starts snapping his head back and forth between me and Mom. He looks at me, clearly wondering if he should go catch me and then looks at Mom trying to figure out if he should help her, and then back to me, then back to Mom, over and over like he's broken. Mom's not even angry, she just reached into her sweatshirt pocket, grabbed a Kleenex out, and casually stuffed it into her nose. Then Mom shakes her head and walks out of the room, yelling something about 'War is war. Just have at each other, but leave me out of it.' It was like a real-life comedy!

"As soon as she's gone, Rudy pounces toward me. Chase time! I run around the house like a crazy chicken until he's winded. Then suddenly he looked at the clock, realized he was late, rushed into the garage, and hopped on his little girl bike with his lunch box in hand, riding into the sunrise to meet his girlfriend. Legit best morning ever! For me, not him."

Becky draws a deep breath and nods her head with resolution, letting me know she's done talking.

"And then? What happened next?"

"Nothing, he just texted me a picture of his chewed-up mashed potato sandwich with the words 'GAME ON, little one!'"

"Huh? He dared to call you little!?" I shriek through laughter.

"Right? As if he could get the true master back!"

*****

Becky and I are waiting all day Thursday for Rudy's revenge. Nothing! I thought for sure my phone would be full of messages after I was done at the rink and with ballet. Not a single text from Becky. We spend the rest of the afternoon plotting our next move and trying to figure out why Rudy didn't attack yet.

"I bet he's run out of ideas!" Becky quips. "We are clearly better at this!"

"Yeah, if he didn't get us back already, it's probably safe to assume he surrenders. Do you want to attack again, or accept his truce?"

"Accept his truce?" Becky asks boldly. "Ha! Never! I'll accept his surrender though!"

"I vote we attack one more time so he knows he's in over his head!"

"That's not a bad idea. Like the attacking of Japan in World War II. Our country chose to prove that we could annihilate their entire land so they would understand that a surrender was necessary. Although that's a tragic story, so maybe we should go a bit more gentle on Rudy."

"A bit!? A lot more gentle! Becky! You can't actually bomb your brother, you know!" I blurt out.

"I suppose you're right. At the end of the day, he's pretty all right I guess."

Becky and I continue to plot our next prank, making lists of ideas—everything from swapping his toothpaste with soap, sewing the bottom of his pants together so he can't put his leg in, and even filling his entire bedroom with balloons so he can't get through the door! I can't wait until tomorrow when we decide which prank to use and make our plans!

CHAPTER 20

Bare Feet

*D**ing.*

Ding.

Ding.

I twist my blankets across my body tighter in an effort to pull them over my head. I'm so sore from yesterday's off-ice ballet class; I don't even want to move!

Ding.

What is going on? My phone is lighting up next to me with messages galore, and as the dinging continues, I quickly realize that I need to respond if I want to make it stop!

Groaning, I reach for my phone: 6:43 a.m. Who on earth is texting me? Becky. Of course.

> Khalli! Omg he's clever…and so very mean! I thought he was done when he didn't get us back all day yesterday. I take it all back! He's not "pretty alright!"
>
> Khalli, I need you to help me!
>
> What size shoe do you wear?

You absolutely NEED to respond
before you leave for the rink!!!
Khalli? Shoe size!
Are you up? Can I come over?

It's too early to have any idea what Becky is talking about.

I'm still sleeping. Maybe later.

I text back and roll back into my pillow.
Ding.
Ding.
Seriously?

What?!?

I reply, clearly irritated. Tossing my phone down on my pillow, I grab my water bottle off the nightstand. Might as well get a start on today's hydration if I'm going to be up now. "Thanks, Becky," I mutter to myself before taking a drink.

I need to know your shoe size. And I
need to borrow a pair. My shoes are all missing! Every single pair! Rudy's a monster!

I spit my entire mouthful of water out in shock. Who would have expected that? It's kind of brilliant.

Wow!

I text back, not knowing what else to say.

Yeah, I know. But don't compliment the enemy. So can I borrow a pair of shoes? Flip flops even?

Sure, come over. I'll unlock the front door.

I rapidly text back.

Less than thirty seconds later, Becky is already inside my house, barefoot. I can't help but burst out in laughter at her panicked face and naked feet.

"Not funny, Khalli!"

I dash up to my room, Becky in tow. "I think I'm a size 5. Borrow whatever. I just need a pair to get to the rink."

We open my closet door, and "Oh no!" I nearly scream. "They're gone! They are all gone! Every single shoe!"

Becky and I race to the mudroom where I usually have a pair or two left behind. Gone! Rudy took my shoes too! He must have known Becky was going to borrow mine.

"Hey, girls! You're up early!" Mom walks into the mudroom with a cup of tea in hand and a mischievous grin painted on her face.

"What do you know? Help us! Our shoes are missing!"

Mom's eyes shimmer with pleasure. "I know that the enemy of my enemy is my friend. I needed to get you back for the mashed potatoes, and the perfect opportunity presented itself. I'd have to be a fool not to take it! Rudy has such a creative mind, don't you think?"

"Huh? You're conspiring with Rudy? Against your own daughter? How could you!"

"More or less the same way that I conspired with my daughter against Rudy, only this time I knew I was participating. It's way more fun when I know what I'm doing!" Mom lets out an evil snicker before sharply turning and heading into the kitchen.

"Mom!" I race behind her into the kitchen, Becky at my heels.

"Auntie Krista! This is beyond evil!" Becky rages. "Like, way more evil than feeding my brother your delicious mashed potatoes. They were *so* good! Just like you, Auntie Krista. Deep down inside, you want to be good! And you *want* to tell us where our shoes are!"

"Oh, Becky, you're so right. I really do want to tell you where your shoes are. I almost feel a bit bad seeing your cold, naked toes right now."

"It's okay..." Becky nearly whimpers. "My feet will be fine once you help us!"

Got her! Becky mouths at me behind my mom's back.

Thank goodness! I can't handle not having any shoes; how will I get to the rink?

"Okay, let me know how I can help," Mom says full of cheer.

"All we need is for you to tell us where you and Rudy hid our shoes! Easy! Then you save the day and become our hero!"

"I would love to be your hero!" Mom smiles.

Becky's right; we got her! This was too easy!

"But..." Mom stammers.

"But what?" I nearly throw my hands in the air!

"But...Rudy's a pro. He knows I can be soft, so we agreed the best plan was simply for me to collect the shoes and give them all to him. That way, when you girls got all cute, like now..." She pauses. "I wouldn't spoil the prank. And it was a darn good prank!" she nearly shouts, laughing. "Good luck, girls! And like I'd actually help you after you tricked me! Ha! Gotcha!"

Becky and I huff at my mom, perfectly in sync. She just played us!

"But, Mom! How am I going to get to the rink?"

"Well..." Mom pauses. "Since it's Friday and you don't have off-ice classes, you can just wear your skates to the rink with your guards."

"Seriously?" I fold my arms across my chest.

"Seriously! Now have a great day, ladies!" And she turns to leave the room, nearly skipping all the way. Mom is really enjoying this.

*****

Becky and I spend nearly an hour searching each of our homes in our bare feet. No luck!

"That's it, I'm texting Rudy! I'm over this!"

Becky whips out her phone and smashes away at the screen, texting as hard as I've ever seen.

> Rudy! This is getting ridiculous! Where are our shoes?!?!

Near-immediate response from Rudy; he must have been waiting for Becky.

> I agree—this is getting ridiculous. It's time to stop. So, every day that you don't prank me, I'll give you and Khalli each one shoe back.

> One? One pair, you mean!

> Nope. One shoe. Welcome to the end of our war—I'm proclaiming victory.

"I'm so getting him back!" Becky screams.

"No, you're not! I need my shoes back! Becky! We need to stop, at least for now! It's going to take over a week to get all our shoes back!"

"Ugh! I know! You're right, but I don't want to lose!"

"We have to. In order to win, we lose too much, like our dignity in public when we can't go into a store barefoot!"

"Oh no, you're right! No shopping until we get our shoes back! No shoes, no service!" Becky wags her finger at me, pretending to be a salesperson.

I can't even! I bust out laughing. This may be miserable, but at least Becky and I are in it together! We agree to end the war…for now, and I head home to wash the dirt off my bare feet so I can put my skates on and head to the rink.

CHAPTER 21

Stay on Your Path

I scurry into the rink at the last minute; there's no point arriving early if I'm already wearing my skates. I have thirty minutes to warm up and practice before my lesson with Coach Marie.

I use my Skating Skills test patterns to get warm before moving on to jumps. Hopefully my achy body will stop hurting once it's warm. I know Coach Marie wanted to work on my skills today, but I've been so close on my Axel that I'd like to show her. Maybe if I'm already working on it when it's time for my lesson, my coach will let me do some in our lesson.

I set up on the hockey line and start pounding my Axels, one after another, after another. And talk about a pounding! My body slams into the ice over and over again. Ugh! As if I wasn't sore enough!

About fifty failed attempts later, Coach Marie skates up to me as I'm dragging my fatigued body off the ice yet again.

"Hey! I love the effort, Khalli! But the longer you jump today, the sloppier your technique is getting. It's probably best to give yourself a break."

"I don't want a break. I want to land this. So badly! And I'm working so hard." I stumble through my frustrations with a quivering voice. "I don't get it. I work on this jump all the time. I practice at home, on the ice, I do all the practice exercises, but still I can't land it. Do you think I'll ever land it? Maybe I should quit... Do you think?" I practically stutter the last line out through my emerging emotions. I just cannot understand what I'm doing wrong.

Coach Marie looks at me firmly, not a trace of empathy in her face. "Khalli, do you truly believe that I'm going to let you fail?"

I shoot her a look. I don't even know how to respond. I think I was expecting a little empathy, or at least a soft reaction. I just continue to fail, slamming my body into the ice one jump after another, and this is her response?

Coach Marie looks me in the eyes. "How long did it take you to learn to write?" I don't respond. "How long until you could hold a pencil in your hand?" My coach is waiting for an answer.

"I don't know, kindergarten maybe."

"Okay, and then how much longer before you could spell?"

I shrug.

"How old were you when you could write a sentence, and then a paragraph, and then a paper?"

I think I see where my coach is going with this.

"It's a process, Khalli. If you want to be able to do something, you have to work at it. I can't just hand you your Axel. I can teach you the skills, but you have to apply them. And you have to apply them over and over until your body figures it out. And your body is figuring it out, and rather quickly I must say! You've been putting in such great effort. Now trust the process. As the skills get harder, the amount of time it takes to learn them gets longer as well."

I nod, almost a bit ashamed that I asked. "But what about Tamerah? I heard her telling someone that she landed her Axel on the first day."

"That's true, but did she tell you how long she worked to perfect it? She landed it, but it was a mess. Sure, you didn't land yours yet, but your positions are beautiful. And when you do land it, I don't think you're going to have nearly as much to clean up. You can't compare yourself to others, Khalli. Maybe the end goal is the same, but the road there is different for everyone. Stay on your path. You'll get there. I promise."

Coach Marie goes over some Axel technique with me, and we do a few more together before she calls enough. "I want you to save your energy, Khalli. I know landing the Axel is important to you, and I agree that it's a very important skill. But there's a deadline approaching for a test session at the end of the summer, and I think preparing for that should be your priority for today's lesson."

I kind of figured we'd still carry out Coach Marie's plans for today, but at least she let me do a few Axels, even if it did mean that I got a bit frustrated. In the end, she helped me feel better about the process. I know she's right; I need to trust that she won't let me fail.

After my lesson and practice, I sit down in the lobby and start to take off my skates. As soon as I unlace and yank the left skate off my foot, I realize I don't have shoes because of Rudy's prank. Ugh! I slide my steamy foot back into my moist, sweaty skate and pull my guards over my blades again. This couldn't be any more uncomfortable. I can't wait to get in the car to finally take my skates off!

CHAPTER 22

If the Shoe Fits

Saturday morning, I wake up to one white-and-green Adidas sneaker. Just one. "Rudy!" I scream with my full wrath at absolutely no one!

Mom shakes her head. "No need to be mad. He kept his word."

Ugh!

We have no family plans today, and I can't exactly go anywhere with only one shoe. So I message Becky to see if she wants to have a barefoot movie marathon day.

> Not really. I'm too antsy and irritated
> with my brother winning the war to sit still.
> How about a makeover day instead?

> You know it's not a real war, right?

I reply and then immediately follow with,

Sure—but only if we can paint our nails.

Duh! I'll be over in 30 minutes. I still have to shower. And this war is real to me!!

Thirty minutes—shoot! I have to eat breakfast and shower too. And then sort through my makeup for our makeovers!

After I get out of the shower, I unlock my phone to a dozen texts. All from Becky.

Keeloni just texted me. Care if she joins?

Oh and Tanja, too!

Well—if this is going to be a party, Dacia should be here, too. I'll text her.

Okay Dacia's coming, too now!

Can we all come to your house? If not, mom said we can hang out here. But I'd rather not because…RUDY!

Hey! Khalli! Where'd you go? They'll be here in an hour. Can we all come over?

Well, my lame Saturday just got way more exciting!

"Mom! Please!" I beg after asking if all my friends can come to our house.

"I mean, it's kind of hard for me to say no when Rudy basically grounded you. So sure. As long as you promise to stay upstairs or outside. I have a lot of work to do today."

"Yes!" I screech as I bolt up the steps to organize my room to make a bit more space for makeovers. Today is going to turn out all right, and by tomorrow, I'll have two shoes and can return to normal life.

*****

I'm still drying my hair after my shower when the door-bell rings. I know it's not Becky because she would come in without knocking. Tossing my towel on the hook, I race down the steps to get the door.

"Hey, Tanja! Come in. I'm not ready yet but will be soon!"

Before Tanja can step into our house, Tylisa jumps out of the car and races up behind her.

"Khalli! Guess what?" Tylisa is calling before I can even greet her.

I don't even have time to respond before she announces, "I get to take skating lessons! At your rink! I'm a figure skater too now!"

Tylisa sprints up to me and wraps her arms around my waist. "Thank you for teaching me. I loved it! I get to start next month!"

I can't stop smiling at Tylisa! "It's the best sport ever. You're going to love it!" I tell her as I hug her back.

"Oh, I already do!" She giggles as she runs back to the car.

"You know she's in love with skating because she really looks up to you, right?" Tanja tells me. "She couldn't stop talking about her lesson with you and everything you could do. She completely adores you!"

Wow! I'm not even sure how to respond. I had no idea I could have such an impact on someone younger than me, and someone I've only met a few times!

Tanja's burst of loud laughter at Becky as she hobbles down the sidewalk with one shoe on takes me away from my thoughts.

"Just go barefoot!" Tanja yells.

"No way! I'm trying to show the entire neighborhood how evil my brother can be!"

"Well, it sounds like war to me, and all is fair in love and war!" Tanja laughs.

"Ugh!" Becky and I both mutter in unison.

"Come on! Let's go inside. My bare feet are cold!" I insist.

Just as Becky and Tanja enter my room, the doorbell rings. All three of us spin around and bolt to the front door to Dacia and Keeloni together.

"I hitched a ride!" Keeloni smiles as she waves to Dacia's brother as he backs out of the driveway.

"So how do I hitch a ride?" Becky winks. "Your brother is the absolute cutest!"

Dacia shakes her head in disgust. "Ew."

We all scurry up to my room for an afternoon of make-overs, girl talk, and ridiculous amounts of fun.

"Let's start with you, Khalli! Since your hair is still wet, it's time to dry and style it. I would love to put you in braids!" Keeloni exclaims, reaching for my wet, dark-blonde strands.

"I would absolutely love braids!"

And the fun begins!

CHAPTER 23

Mismatched

The sun beats through my pastel curtains as I ignore my Sunday morning alarm. I am so tired from yesterday's fun with my friends! I reach over to silence my alarm and can't help but smile when I notice my neon-green and hot-pink fingernails—this is what happens when I let Becky pick the colors! I like them, but they are a bit louder than what I would have chosen on my own; I'll really need to be creative to find an outfit that matches for church!

I drag my exhausted body downstairs, motivated by the smell of mom's fresh homemade waffles; this is a breakfast worth getting up early for!

"Rudy left you a gift on your seat," Mom says, nearly snickering.

My shoe! I skip to the table and pull out my chair, only to find a pink flip-flop.

"What?" I nearly screech.

Mom smiles. "Rudy was really considerate. He said he talked to Becky about your makeover party, and she said your nails were pink and green. He decided to do his best to help you match. And now you have a right flip-flop to go with the left Adidas shoe!"

"You're kidding, right?" I grumble, knowing fully that she's not.

Mom smiles. "He's keeping his word. Now onto breakfast! We have to leave for church in about thirty minutes."

"I can't go with mismatched shoes!"

"Well, you're going. So you can choose between bare feet, mismatched shoes, or you can wear some of my shoes which are going to be just a bit too big," Mom offers, almost sympathetically.

I don't even need to think about that. "I'll wear yours. Thank you, Mom!"

Mom nods, and I eat my breakfast calmly, thankful that I won't have to show up to church in one flip-flop and one sneaker.

*****

Monday morning, I woke up grateful to a second tennis shoe. I text Becky right away.

Finally, two shoes that match!

My phone dings nearly as soon as I set it down.

Lucky you! I apparently have three left feet. Rudy hates me!

I swallow. Poor Becky! Rudy is really torturing her.

I'm sorry—want to borrow a right pink
flip flop?

Yes! I'll be there in 30 seconds!

Becky bursts through my door in less than a minute; she's barefoot with a red flip-flop for her left foot in hand. "I don't even care if they match! At least I can go into public. Apparently, no shoes, no service really is a thing. I got kicked out of the mini-mart yesterday!"

I can't help but laugh at Becky as she's shaking her head in frustration. As miserable as the first two days were, at least we were in it together! Now I have a pair of shoes, and Becky is still left struggling to go into public—rough!

Becky leaves with her mismatched flip-flops while I get ready for the rink. I hear her venting to my mom on her way out the door and can't help but laugh at how ridiculous this entire prank war has become.

CHAPTER 24

Confused and Amused

"Let's go! Let's go! C'mon!" Coach Marie is yelling as she chases us down the ice. Tuesday power class is intense! "Bend your knees! Push! Let's go!"

I find I'm doing a better job surviving this class than the first one, and the drills are even more intense. Coach Jessica was right; this is going to make me stronger. In fact, I'm apparently already stronger!

"Alternating lunges! Stay down in your knees! I don't want to see you rising. Stay engaged! Let's go!" my coach yells, and we push from one lunge into the next over and over again. My thighs are burning!

I look to Yana and see pure focus in her eyes. Sweat drips from her hairline and down the side of her face; she is clearly giving 100 percent.

I see a similar drive in Coach Jessica, Stacy, Tamera, and Mila. Everyone is pouring their full energy into their lunges. My legs throb. My lungs burn. My mouth feels dry from breathing in the cold air so aggressively. How many more?

"Again!" my coach yells.

We all push through another set.

"Again!"

I literally do not think I can do any more. I'm burning up, dripping in sweat.

"Again!"

I put every ounce of remaining strength I have into the lunges. There's no way I can continue after this set. I glance at the others; they all look like they are going to pass out, but their determination radiates through their fierce gazes and powerful pushes.

"Again!"

I think I might die.

"Again! Last one! You can do this! Let's go!"

I give it everything I've got, and I make it!

"One lap and then a water break. Nice job, guys! You just proved how strong you really are. Not only to me, I already knew, but to yourselves. Way to go!"

My coach is right. As miserable as this was, I just learned my limits go far beyond what I thought they would.

After class, I have fifteen minutes during the Zamboni break to cool down before my practice ice. I am dripping in sweat.

"You smell gross."

I snap around to see Mila's face staring at me. Who else would it be? I open my mouth to respond, but she cuts me off.

"But so do I. You really are a hard worker, Khalli. I know I wasn't exactly nice to you before, but...um...I guess I'm saying I'm sorry."

I bust out laughing, and Mila's face immediately tightens.

"Wait, sorry!" I stop myself. "I'm laughing because I've never had anyone start an apology with 'You smell gross.' It's like something my best friend would say. I thought you were going to insult me, but I believe you just gave me a compliment. It's just the most interesting apology I've ever heard, that's all. But, of course, I accept! And I'm sorry that I was mean to you too."

She nods.

"And you definitely do smell bad too," I add with a grin.

"Then even though you just laughed in my face at my apology, I'll accept," Mila says half-snickering.

We tilt our heads at each other, clearly confused and amused, and suddenly both giggle.

"I think we should talk more," I finally say.

"I think that could maybe work. Just not on the ice," Mila states.

"Deal." I nod as Mila walks away.

"Well, that was the most awkward conversation I've ever heard!" Stacy giggles from behind me as she laces her skates up again. "But it's cool that you two are getting along. Someone had to break the ice."

I nod. That was definitely an odd conversation, but I'm amused enough that I plan to talk to Mila again. And sooner than later.

CHAPTER 25

Let the Planning Begin!

The rest of the week keeps me plenty busy between skating and summer fun. This week's mission: plan the perfect eleventh birthday party! My birthday is August 6, and I want my friends to have enough time to clear their calendars; but before I can send out invitations, I need a theme!

"A manicure party?" Becky suggests Thursday afternoon after days of brainstorming. She's even wearing matching shoes today for the first time since Rudy stole all of them.

"I feel like we do manicure and makeover parties all the time."

"I know, and they are so fun!" Becky exclaims.

"I want something different for my birthday."

"Unicorns and sprinkles?" she says, cocking her head to the side half-joking, half-serious.

I giggle, shaking my head.

"11! Two ones don't make a right! Get it? Like two wrongs? Everything has to have one in it. One-der bread sandwiches, music by One Direction, and other bands with 'One' in the name. One...um..."

"*One* more suggestion like that, and I'll fire you from my planning committee!" I bust out laughing.

"Okay, fine. What were you thinking?"

"I was thinking maybe having a skating theme."

"Like an ice-skate-shaped cake?"

"That's a great idea!" I exclaim. "And maybe everyone gets a party gift of skate guards!"

Becky scrunches her face. "I don't think a lot of your friends will have a use for that. But what if you merge skating with dancing? I'd take a hot-pink tutu!"

My jaw drops. "That's a great idea! Not the tutu, the dancing! What if we use my birthday party to learn a dance together? At the end, I send everyone the video of our dance!"

"That sounds exhausting!" Becky laughs. "But it's your birthday, and it could be fun. Maybe we just dance to a short song though. Otherwise it's going to take all day."

"Done! A skating-dance birthday party!"

"Ooh, how about movement instead? Moving on to eleven, or moving through the years?" Becky bursts with excitement at her idea.

"Well, it's better than 'Two ones don't make a right!'" I laugh. "I'll think about it."

*****

I love Friday lessons with Coach Marie. I work so hard all week, and on Fridays I get to show her my progress and get helpful corrections. I've made some really good progress on my Axel—*At least*, I think—and cannot wait to get her feedback.

We start with my Skating Skills patterns. "I really want to work on your backward crossovers today. This test uses them in multiple patterns, plus they are so important in free skate."

I show Coach Marie my back crossovers on the center circle.

"These are getting so much better, Khalli! I love your power! I just want to make some adjustments to your posture. Can you feel yourself leaning forward?"

I guess now that I think about it, I'm aware I am. I nod.

Coach Marie helps adjust my posture, getting me to lean more into my back shoulder. This is way more uncomfortable!

"I promise it'll get easier the more you do it," she encourages me after seeing the discomfort in my face. "Now keep your hips under you!"

Ugh! I'm leading with my butt again! I push my hips under me; lift up my rib cage, as Coach Marie has directed so many times; and sit back into my shoulder.

"So much better! Now turn your head to look behind you," she orders.

I adjust.

"Yes, Khalli!" she encourages as I push powerfully around the circle multiple times. "Let's do the other direction. Put it in your test pattern, and then we'll go on to free skate!"

I grin at my coach. I cannot wait to work on my Axel! It's time to focus so we can move on to free skate!

CHAPTER 26

Maybe Mila

"Let's make a list of who's coming to your birthday party. Let's plan for five or six friends max," Mom tells me Saturday morning.

"Okay. I want to invite Becky, Dacia, Tanja, and Keeloni of course." Mom scribbles their names down and nods. "Perfect."

"Wait, I'm not done!"

"Well, that's already four. If you want a sleepover, we really don't have much more room."

"Mom! We're sleeping in a tent outside. If we run out of room, I'll just ask for another tent for my birthday."

"Well then!" Mom exclaims at my sass. "Let's hear the rest of your list."

"Stacy and Yana for sure, and I was also thinking maybe Mila."

"Maybe Mila?" Mom raises an eyebrow.

"I want to give her a chance. She might not come anyway, but it seems like the right thing to do if I'm inviting Yana and Stacy."

Mom softens. "That's really mature of you, Khalli." Then after a thoughtful pause, "Are you sure Yana and Stacy will want to come? They are a bit older than you and your school friends."

"They can always say no. And Yana is only two years older than me, and Stacy is only a year-and-a-half older than her. But even so, they are my friends. I want to do a skating and dance-themed party, so I think they'll be interested."

"So you're inviting seven people? That's a bit more than five or six," Mom hints. "How old is Mila?"

"Mila is actually only a year older than me. She's competed against Yana forever as rivals."

"This birthday party sounds like drama. Count me out! If you think you can keep everyone busy enough to get along, I'm going to let you make it happen, but I do not want any arguing."

"I know, Mom, but this is my chance to maybe get my rink family back and to see everyone get along. I want that more than anything! And I want all my friends to meet."

My mom nods coolly, clearly a little concerned. "I haven't met Mila's parents yet. Maybe I'll invite them to join me for a cup of tea at the start of your party so they feel better about leaving Mila for a sleepover."

I smile at my mom; this means she'll be busy and out of the way at the beginning of my party!

*****

I spend the majority of the weekend party planning with Becky. I'm the last of all my friends to turn eleven and cannot wait for this party!

I've decided the theme will be "11!" and I'm going to draw each of the ones as an upright skate blade. I've searched online and found ice skate cupcake decorations; so Mom will bake the cupcakes, and Becky and I will decorate.

"Chocolate and vanilla! Ooh, and red velvet!" Becky exclaims when I tell her my plan.

"Mom asked me to choose one flavor, but I'll see what I can do! After all, it is my birthday!" I hint with a wink.

We move onto planning the activities.

"I want to pick a song and all create a dance together! We'll record it and then watch it together. Keeping the video will make a cool memory!"

"That sounds like so much work. But it's your party, so game on! Before we do anything though, we should start by setting up the tent together. If we wait too long and it gets dark out, it's going to be way harder."

"You're not wrong!" I agree. "And we both know Mom is not going to let us sleep inside, especially with eight of us!"

"Eight?"

"Yeah! You and me, of course. And then Dacia, Tanja, and Keeloni. And then Yana, Stacy, and Mila."

"Who are Stacy and Mila? Yana is your friend at the rink. I'm excited to meet her, but who are the others? What kind of secret life are you living that you haven't told me about?" Becky half-pouts and half-scolds me with her final question.

I tell her the entire situation.

"I know I can't get mad that you have other friends because when Dacia and I made other friends, you got to know them, and we all got along. But it is a bit weird to me that you're so close to people that I've never met."

"That's why I want to invite them! I want all my friends to know each other and get along."

"I hope we do. This drama with Mila sounds like at the very least your birthday party will be interesting!"

I really hope Becky and my mom are wrong about the drama. I just want everyone to get along.

CHAPTER 27

Determined

"Hi, Khalli!" Coach Marie greets me on the ice Monday morning. "Have you warmed up your jumps yet?"

"I have." I grin; I live for jump lessons! "I warmed them up off-ice in the lobby and also on-ice. And I've been doing my Axel off-ice every single day. It's getting easier for me!"

My coach nods. "I love your dedication. Let's see what your jumps look like today! How about we start with a couple loop jumps and move forward from there?"

"Okay," I eagerly reply over my shoulder, already skating off to show my coach a loop jump.

"Your shoulders are rotating ahead of the rest of your body," my coach calls as I land.

Shoot! "I can fix it!" I respond back without coming to a stop. I buzz right past my coach and set up for a second loop jump. I check my right shoulder behind me and set my left arm. As I jump, I take extra care to keep my right shoulder back rather than letting it swing around me.

"So much better! Now look to the right on your landing!" my coach yells out, and I turn my head on command.

"Nice, Khalli. Let's move on."

We work on my flip and Lutz jumps before moving onto the Axel. For the Axel, we practice some walk-throughs. I show my coach my practice exercise on the boards where she has me step up off the ice, transferring my weight over my right side. Once she's convinced my technique is where it needs to be, we go for the jump on the hockey line.

I tell her all the things I'm supposed to be thinking about before she lets me try the jump: things like keeping my right side back, not hinging forward at the hips, jumping out of my circle rather than around to the left. Once she's convinced I'm ready, she lets me try my first full Axel of the day, and then immediately after, she reaches her hand down to help me up off the ice.

"Not bad, Khalli. But you pulled yourself over your right side too quickly. I want you to wait for your right foot to pass through in front of you and then climb over your right side, just like we did in the exercise on the wall."

"Can we do the exercise one more time before I jump again? I want to feel my weight transferring and see if I can then feel it in my jump."

"Absolutely!" Coach Marie follows me to the door at the hockey box. I step up off the ice with my right foot and set it on the raised rubber floor. Next, I push my weight forward up beyond the toes of my left foot and rotate counterclock-wise as I snap over my right foot, creating the perfect air position over my right side.

"Very well done, Khalli! I love how you kept your hips under you on the snap. Would you like to do a couple more before you try this action in the jump again?"

I nod and proceed to do three more at the boards.

Feeling confident, I stroke back to the hockey line, and without saying a word to Coach Marie, I commit to the jump. Up, over the right side, stay over the right side, and my right blade hits the ice, followed a millisecond later by my left foot which is still crossed over the top. But I'm still standing!

"Khalli! That was it! You just need to check out now!"

My coach, her hazel eyes shining, throws me a high five and guides me over to the boards where we walk through the checkout. I really work at sharply lifting my left leg up and punching it out. "Include your head in this exercise," my coach orders. "If you're working on the landing, you should be working on the *entire* landing."

I do as she asks multiple times before telling her I'm ready. I land two more with my foot crossed in the landing.

"You've got this, Khalli! You need to commit to the landing."

I nod sternly. I know I can do this. It's time to commit.

I launch myself into the jump again, waiting for my right foot to pass through before pulling tight over my right side. Then I pull my left knee up to open my position and punch my left leg back for the landing. Where's the ice? I hold my position; it's got to be down there somewhere. *Boom!* My right hip smashes full force into the rock-hard ice. I just lay right where I landed, afraid it's going to hurt too much to move.

"Khalli!" Coach Marie crouches next to me.

"I'm fine," I utter before she can say anymore. "I just need a minute. Can you tell me what I did wrong while I lay here?"

"I will tell you what you did wrong as soon as you're standing again, but take a moment if you need it. What hurts the most, your right hip?"

I nod as I scrape my body off the ice. "I'm fine. I just wasn't expecting that…"

"You pre-rotated your takeoff, Khalli. You need to jump out of your circle. Try taking your arms slightly to the right when you slice them forward. They will help guide your body outward." She demonstrates with her arms.

"Oh, that makes sense. Okay." I set up for another Axel before I can be told no, and land once again on two feet.

"Let's try this, Khalli. I want you to do an Axel-toe loop."

"But that's harder than an Axel alone."

"But think about how safe you'll feel punching out and reaching back if you know your left foot is right there to catch you for the upcoming toe loop."

"I do like that thought." I smile. "Okay."

"Before you do it," Coach Marie stops me mid-push, "make sure you land your Axel with your right shoulder back to set you up for the toe loop."

I nod as I set up again to attempt this combo. Right side back, right leg through, snap over the right side. Then to exit, lift the left knee, and punch back with my left arm in front—right heel through, toe loop. Done.

"Oh my goodness, Khalli!" My coach is racing at me, arms wide open, and embraces me in the biggest hug. "You did it! You just did it! A beautiful Axel-toe combo!"

"I did?" I stutter. "I did! Oh my God, I did! I landed my Axel!"

I'm jumping up and down, still wrapped in Coach Marie's arms. I actually did it! This is literally the best day ever!

We do about ten more, and I land three of them—two of which Coach Marie caught on video. "I'll send these to your mom so you can watch them and show them off. You should be so proud of yourself, Khalli!"

"I am," I say through a gaping smile. "Thank you for helping me!"

Coach Marie gives me another excited hug, and we move on to my program.

CHAPTER 28
The Perfect Invite

The rest of the week has had ups and downs with my Axel. Literally ups and downs—lots of falls and hard crashes, but lots of successful landings. I no longer need the toe loop at the end, but I can add it no problem when I want to. Coach Marie warned me that the Axel takes a little while to make consistent. Sometimes skaters land it, and then lose it, and then get it back again. She told me it's a process, but now that I've landed so many, I know what the jump should feel like. I'm determined to push through the struggles to make this jump consistent.

Currently it's the weekend, and it's party-planning central at my house: my eleventh birthday is only three weeks away, and I cannot wait!

I've decided to mix two oldie songs together for my dance theme. The first is, "It's My Party," and the second is, "Girls Just Wanna Have Fun," because you best believe we will be having fun!

For party favors, I'm going off Becky's idea of wanting a hot-pink tutu. Each of my friends will get their own brightly colored tutu to wear for our video. I've already picked out their colors based on what they like to wear and their favorite colors:

Becky: hot pink—that needed to happen!
Dacia: sky blue.
Keeloni: sunshine yellow.
Tanja: neon orange.
Yana: chartreuse green.
Stacy: baby pink.
Mila: turquoise.
And for myself: deep purple.

Mom said I can't order the tutus until everyone has returned their RSVP, but that doesn't mean I can't plan the rest!

My friends will get their party bag shortly after they arrive. It'll have their tutu, some candy, and a pair of over-sized black sunglasses for our dance performance. If we have some downtime while we wait for everyone to arrive, we can do our makeup for the performance, and then it's choreography time!

I thought about choreographing the dance myself, but then thought that wouldn't be as much fun for my friends— plus it'll probably be better with their input.

Next we'll set up the tent before it gets too dark, and then it'll be cake, ice cream, and gift-opening time! After that, truth or dare, and then a scary movie in the tent on Mom's laptop until the sun comes up. I can't wait!

Today my job is to finish the invitations. We bought a box of glitter invitations, and I'm decorating them with stickers and filling in the details. These couldn't be any cuter! I'm planning to hand-deliver the invitations at the rink to Yana, Stacy, and Mila on Monday. For Becky's, I'll just walk down the street as soon as I'm done, and then I'll drop the other three in the mail since I don't have plans to see my other friends for another week.

As soon as I finish the invitations, Mom already asked me to help her with weeding the lawn, so I'm definitely not in a hurry to finish—these are going to be perfect before I give them to my friends!

CHAPTER 29

Maybe

I ended up helping my mom with weeding for about an hour over the weekend. As much as I didn't want to do lawn work, reminding myself of everything my parents do for me encouraged me to hurry my party invitations along to help my mom. I made it fun for myself by doing an off-ice Axel after every five weeds I pulled. Any chance I can get to squeeze in extra practice will help me make my Axel consistent! I think I did about fifty Axels; that's a lot of weeds!

Today I get to have my regular lesson with Coach Marie and can't wait to show her my progress! After warming up and stretching, I start my jumps right away. This Axel will be ready for her!

When my lesson starts, I'm already about twenty Axels in and have landed about half of them! Coach Marie skates over and immediately starts giving me corrections. "Nice height! After you climb over your right leg, remember that you're aiming to line up your nose, belly button, right knee, and right middle toe. This should be your back spin position in the air." Coach Marie demonstrates as she talks.

I continue to jump, Axel after Axel.

"Okay, not bad, Khalli! These are coming along quite nicely. I imagine by the time I see you Friday, you'll be landing the majority."

I smile. That was a compliment from Coach Marie even though most people might not think so. She directs me onto my skills test patterns. "There's a test session here on August 13. I want you to test."

What? That's the week after my birthday—this could turn out to be the best birthday ever!

"You think I'm ready?" I ask.

"Almost. I think most judges would pass your test as it stands now, but I want you to be good enough that *all* judges will pass you. So let's get to work!"

We pound my patterns for the next forty minutes. Coach Marie mostly picks on my hip alignment and toe point. "Your upper body carriage has gotten quite nice, Khalli. If you get your hips under you, I'll be satisfied with this test!"

After my lesson and practice time, I head to the lobby to take my skates off and pass out my birthday invitations! I give one to Stacy, set Yana's in her skate bag since she's busy doing off-ice with Coach Marie during this Zam break, and then head toward Mila.

"Hi," I say cheerfully, stopping in front of her with my skates still on.

"Um, hi," Mila replies without looking up.

I reach her invitation out toward her. "This is for you."

Mila drops her laces and tilts her head toward me, a confused look on her face.

"It's an invitation to my birthday party. We are going to choreograph a dance together! I invited Yana and Stacy as well."

Mila's face is blank, almost like she doesn't know what to say.

"I would love for you to come!" I smile as sincerely as possible. "I still think maybe we can be friends if you want to."

"Maybe. I mean, thank you," Mila replies, looking like she could cry.

I wanted to call her out on her reaction. I just invited you to my birthday party; I only get to invite a limited amount of people, and all you do is say maybe! But something about the way she said thank you made me hesitate. She actually looked really sad.

I sit down across from her and begin to take my skates off. Mila doesn't say anything more but starts to delicately pick at a knot at the end of her lace that looks like it could have been there for weeks, occasionally glancing up at me from the corner of her eye.

"I'm ordering tutus for the dance, a different color for everyone!" I finally say as enthusiastically as I can. "I've picked out a turquoise one for you, but I could order a different color if you'd like."

Mila's head snaps up, her eyes wide. "Turquoise is my favorite color."

"I know." I grin. "Your guards, soakers, water bottle, and phone case are all that color, so I figured you like it."

Mila is now smiling. I've never noticed her dimples before. Actually, I'm not sure if I've even seen her smile before.

"You really put some thought into this, didn't you?"

I nod.

"Okay." She pauses. "I'll see if I'm allowed to come. It depends on my dad's plans, but I probably can't. He doesn't ever want to take me anywhere. He just works all the time, and when he is home, he's exhausted and crabby. So I just stay inside my tiny room all weekend. But I'll ask. Thank you, Khalli. Just that you asked was really nice. Maybe we will be friends someday."

"Maybe we can even be friends right now," I say with a gentle enthusiasm.

"Maybe. I'll ask." And with that, Mila packs up her skates—her knot still fully intact in her lace—and heads toward the door.

CHAPTER 30

Success!

During power class on Tuesday and ballet on Thursday, Mila was slightly less cold toward everyone. I wouldn't say she was friendly, but she didn't go out of her way to insult anyone. She still gave Yana the stare down in class, and Yana still ignored her with grace. Coach Marie was right: there's something going on in Mila's life that she's not talking about.

On Friday, Mila approaches me before getting on the ice.

"My dad said I can go to your party. But he said I have to take the bus. Is there a bus stop near your house? I will try to figure out the route this week."

"Maybe my mom can pick you up?" I offer.

Mila looks surprised. "You'd arrange a ride for me to your party?"

I nod willingly.

"I think that would work. But if not, I'm getting pretty good at taking the bus. I take it to the rink a lot now."

I try my best to hide how shocked I am. My mom would never let me take the bus alone, and Mila is only a year older than me.

"Do you think the other girls will be okay with me coming? I mean, your school friends, but also Stacy and…" She pauses. "Stacy and Yana."

"They haven't said they have a problem. Stacy can't stay for the sleepover because she has to babysit that night, but I imagine Yana won't mind. If she's willing to share her coach, I imagine she's also willing to share a slumber party." I smile.

Mila purses her lips cautiously. "Okay. I just don't want to ruin your party."

I don't know how to respond, so I smile kindly as I turn to head toward the ice.

I've already warmed up my body and my Axels off-ice. Now it's time to do the same on the ice. Coach Marie comes over for my lesson just as I'm wrapping up my Lutz jump. "Nice outside entry edge, Khalli!"

I grin. "Thank you! Can I show you my Axel today? I haven't warmed it up yet, but I'm ready now."

"All right, let's do it!"

I do two quick walk-throughs to remind my mind and body of the motions. Coach Marie gives me a couple of tips, and then I set up for the actual jump.

Entering the jump, I push my weight up through my left toe pick as my right foot climbs ahead of me. As soon as I feel my right foot pass, I push my right leg straight and climb over it. Staying tight and looking slightly to the right, I maintain my position until the checkout. I lift my left knee up to slow my rotation before punching it back, and it's a clean landing!

"Khalli! That was beautiful!" Coach Marie skates over to give me the biggest high five.

"That felt easy! I'd like to do it again."

And I do five more clean Axels in a row.

"I think it's safe to say you've got your Axel, Khalli!" my coach cheers.

"I feel safe in it. Can I add a little more speed?"

My coach nods.

I attempt it with a bit more speed on the hockey line, and success!

"Let's move it to a circle." Coach Marie guides me to the corner hockey circle and walks me through the setup. "Make sure you're keeping your hips under you when you step forward to jump out of the circle."

She demonstrates what she means, and I feel ready enough to try it. My first attempt ends in a massive crash, but I'm so determined that I ignore my instant bruises and try again and again. After three tries, I successfully land it on the circle!

"Can we do more? I know you want to work on my test, but I feel like I've just made a breakthrough and really want to do some more so I can remember what it feels like."

"It's hard for me to say no to that logic. You're on! Let's do ten more!" my coach encourages.

I land eight out of the next ten jumps and am beyond ecstatic! "I think I've got it!" I practically cheer.

"I think you do too!" Coach Marie reaches over to give me another high five.

Today has been a great day!

CHAPTER 31

Preparation

The last couple of weeks have flown by so fast! I've been working like crazy preparing for my second Skating Skills test, which is barely more than a week away. Both Coach Marie and Coach Jessica told me I'm beyond ready, so we've even started training some patterns from the next test!

My Axel is now mostly consistent, and I'm comfortable doing the jump from powerful backward crossovers. We've even started my double Salchow; it's not nearly as scary for me as the Axel was. My goal is to have a consistent double Salchow by the end of the summer; Coach Marie says I'm very capable of making this happen!

My party is this Friday already! Everyone is coming; but Stacy can only stay for a little, and Yana can't sleep over because of morning ice. On Saturdays she skates at 5:00 a.m. I also think maybe they didn't want to hang out with a bunch of younger kids all night long, but I love that they are coming even if only for a little bit. I can't wait for all my friends to meet each other!

Today is Wednesday, and I am ready for my lesson with Coach Jessica. It's a Skating Skills day; with my test coming up so fast, I need to make sure I'm consistently working on my patterns.

"Belly button points at the ice, Khalli! Point your toe and turn it out. At the very least your foot should be flat and parallel to the ice," Coach Jessica calls to me during my spirals.

I make my adjustments with ease and carry on through the entire pattern.

"Khalli, that was great after you made your corrections, but you shouldn't need to be told at this point." Coach Jessica is usually super picky, but this came out much more sternly than usual.

"I'm sorry. I know these things, and I know I can do it correctly. But my head isn't here today. My birthday party is on Friday, and it's literally all I can think about."

"And your test is just over a week away and *needs* to be what you're thinking about when you're on the ice," Coach Jessica replies seriously. "I know how hard you've worked. I know how badly you want this. This is the time to make it happen."

"I know. And thankfully my test is after my party, so I'll be more focused then."

"But your practice is now. And just like Coach Marie always says, practice makes permanent. You need to be practicing exactly the way you're going to test it. And if the first half of your pattern was how your test is going to look, I'm suddenly rather worried."

I swallow. Coach Jessica is right. I need to do a better job focusing.

"I'd like to do the full pattern again to show you I can do it right," I tell her.

"I would like to see that. And, Khalli." She pauses with a calm smile. "Happy birthday."

I skate to my starting position, thinking about how incredibly similar Coach Jessica can be to Coach Marie. I'm pretty lucky to have two coaches who push me to become my absolute best and who refuse to cut me any slack.

I push off into my pattern, thinking about everything I need to do to make my spiral pattern perfect. I can think about my party later; right now, I need to prepare for my test.

CHAPTER 32

Skittles

It's party time! I am up at the crack of dawn (no alarm necessary!) and sprint out of bed to begin decorating. I finished putting the party favor bags together last night for my friends; they are precisely perfect! Each has a tutu, oversized shiny black sunglasses, and a bunch of sugary goodness! Today is going to be so much fun!

In the kitchen, I hang balloons from the light fixtures, drooping them with careful exquisiteness over the kitchen table. I include one balloon of each color to create a rainbow effect. Then I weave steamers in between. Just wait until Mom and Dad wake up and come downstairs for their tea and coffee; they will be so impressed!

In the living room, I add helium balloons and streamers to the lamps, fireplace mantel, and also droop them from the curtain rods.

Now it's time to decorate outside!

We'll be using the deck for our performance, so obviously I need to add streamers galore! I set out poppers filled with biodegradable confetti in a large bowl on the patio furniture.

Confetti will make for the perfect finish of our dance, and it will dissolve itself away so it doesn't hurt the animals who try to eat it; and I also won't have as much to clean up! I'm adding helium balloons along the deck railing as Mom groggily pokes her head out the patio door.

"Khalli, honey, it's 7:00 a.m. What time did you wake up?"

I shrug. I actually have no idea.

"Do you like it?"

"This is the most colorful morning of my life, that's for sure!" Mom says with a sassy smile. "It's definitely a bit more than I was anticipating, but I guess this is what happens when I send you with your father to buy decorations!"

Mom is not wrong about that: Dad always aims to give me the best!

After finishing some final touches, I step back to admire my hard work. The dark-brown deck boards are completely swallowed in color. My bright rainbow balloons are swaying and spinning in the wind; it looks like a Skittles bomb exploded on my deck, and it couldn't possibly be more beautiful! The streamers dance through the breeze, demonstrating nearly as much grace as some of the best skaters on the ice. Perfection! Now it better not rain before tonight!

"Khalli, why don't you come eat some breakfast? Dad picked up apple turnovers from the bakery while you were working."

I love apple turnovers!

I rush into the house to find my parents both holding a single plate together, complete with a candle glowing over my breakfast. Upon seeing my hurried face, they immediately both start to sing. Man, do I love birthdays!

After breakfast, I get ready for the rink. Fridays are my short days at the rink, and I also get a lesson with Coach Marie. If she works me hard enough, maybe I'll be tired enough to take a short nap before my friends come. Tonight is going to be a late night!

*****

At the rink, Coach Marie says she has a birthday present for me.

"How do you know it's my birthday?"

"Had Coach Jessica not told me about your distractions on Wednesday"—she scrunches her face, showing her disappointment—"then I would have likely figured it out from Yana and Stacy talking in the lobby. Or if not from them, then very possibly from Mila who asked what I thought you'd like for a gift. It appears the entire rink is aware it's your birthday!" Coach Marie jokes.

"Mila was worried about what to get me?" I try to hide the shock from my voice.

Coach Marie nods. "It makes me so happy to see you helping her fit in here, Khalli. After how things started this summer…I just want you to know I noticed your efforts and am both proud and grateful for everything you're doing to help Mila make Berger Lake her home."

I smile; there are few things better than making my coach proud!

We work through my jumps, and I nail a ton of Axels, one after the next—now that's my kind of birthday!

"Aren't you curious about your birthday present, Khalli?"

I nod anxiously. "I really am!"

"Your birthday present is…" She pauses for effect. "We are going to start double toe loops."

"Seriously?" I can't help but bounce up and down. My birthday really is the best day ever!

CHAPTER 33

The Party Begins

"*Khaaalli!* This is *maaagical!*" Becky draws out upon entering my home.

Becky's head tilts up toward the ceiling as she turns in a slow circle admiring my decorating skills.

"Whoa!" She steps back, losing her balance after one too many spins. "I'm definitely not a figure skater like you!" She giggles as she finds her center again.

Becky came a bit earlier than everyone else to help me get ready.

"I've just decided: you're getting a birthday rainbow manicure in honor of your completely amazing decorations! And I brought nail polish so we'll have all the colors!" She lifts her plastic beauty chest by the handle in front of my face.

"Just decided, huh?" I giggle. Becky clearly decided she was giving me a manicure before she arrived.

"What? I brought this for later. In case we need some chill time for makeovers around midnight."

Becky pulls me by my hand up the stairs to my room and proceeds to put three to four colors of paint on each of my fingernails. "It's an experiment, but if the colors don't mush together too much, it'll look amazing." she exclaims with confidence as she decorates my nails.

Becky curls my hair while my nails are drying. "The birthday girl needs a little extra bounce!" She giggles, pulling my fresh curl downward until it's straight and then releasing it so it bounces back up. "You are supposed to have the best hair here since it's your party, and I'm going to make sure of it!" She boasts of her own skill.

Becky is adding a clear coat to my rainbow nails (which turned out amazing by the way!) as the doorbell rings. "*Ah!*" she screeches, turning her head toward my bedroom door. "I'm not done yet! *Wait!*"

"Now hold still!" she practically shouts as she snaps her head back to me. "Twenty more seconds and we'll have perfection."

We don't even need to get up to get the door because we immediately hear footsteps pounding up the staircase. My dad must have let someone in.

Keeloni and Tanja bolt into my room. "Oh, I love your nails!" Keeloni exclaims.

"Thanks!" Becky answers before I can even respond. "Maybe later tonight I can do yours!"

"No need." Keeloni holds her hand up. "My mom and I had a mother-daughter day on Wednesday and got matching manicures. Look! Flamingos and polka dots!"

We all swoon over Keeloni's pink nails, but secretly I like my rainbow nails by Becky better. What can I say, the girl knows what I like!

*****

Within five minutes we hear the garage door opening; that must be my mom with Mila!

"C'mon, guys, let's go greet Mila! She's never been here before, so she might be nervous," I encourage the others to follow as I sprint down the stairs.

Becky, directly behind me, grumbles under her breath half-jokingly, "Can't wait to meet the girl that no one likes."

I whip around without hesitation. "This is my birthday, and I want her here. I would love it if my best friend made her feel like she fit in."

Becky's face immediately goes soft. "I'm sorry, Khalli. I'll try."

I give her a quick hug, and we begin our race once again through the house to the garage to get Mila.

The normally fierce and outspoken Mila looks incredibly shy next to my mom as she climbs out of the car.

"I'm so glad you came!" I squeal, attempting to let her know that I really mean it.

With her head down but her eyes looking up with hesitation, she thanks me for inviting her.

I smile. "This is my best friend, Becky. Becky, this is Mila." They awkwardly wave at each other as I reach for

Mila's sleeping bag to help. Becky grabs her pillow, and we head into the house, piling her stuff on top of everyone else's in the living room.

"Oh no!" Mom announces after seeing our pile. "This is an outdoor sleepover!"

"I know. I promise as soon as everyone else arrives, we'll start to move it to the tent, but if we're outside setting up now, the others might feel weird coming in since neither Yana nor Stacy have been here before."

Mom nods, accepting my logic, and Mila cautiously follows Becky and me upstairs to meet the others.

CHAPTER 34

It's My Party

Putting the tent up was a lot of work! It's a supersized tent with three separate rooms; we pulled the dividers back so we could have one massive room for everyone. Most of my friends had never put up a tent this big before! Becky and I are both tent masters, so we ended up doing most of the work. And success! The tent is standing and staked into the ground.

We spread out all our sleeping bags. Since Stacy and Yana are leaving earlier, we only need space for six to sleep; this tent is so huge that there is still plenty of room. Dad gave me two lanterns which we hung from the ceiling. We also have three other flashlights for trips into the house to use the bathroom or to make faces glow for scary stories; we are set!

Now it's time to party!

I sneak away to the porch to grab the tutus and prance back to the tent just in time to hear everyone asking each other where I'd gone. I bolt in and start launching the tutus at my friends. "Becky!" I shout, firing the hot-pink tutu straight toward her open arms!

"You weren't kidding about the pink tutu!" She laughs.

I'm already tossing the yellow tutu toward Keeloni but sneak Becky a wink before setting the light blue tutu on Dacia's head as she sits down on the ground next to me.

Before the tutus are in everyone's hands, Tanja is already changing into her all-black outfit. "I've figured it out! I thought we were going to do some sort of ninja pranking in the middle of the night when you requested an all-black outfit, but looking at Becky in her tutu over black, you clearly have more exciting plans!"

Stepping into my eggplant-purple tutu, I can't help but smile. I definitely have more exciting plans!

My friends follow me to the porch where I explain my plans to create a dance video. Yana, Stacy, and Mila seem pretty excited; as skaters, they are definitely used to performing. Tanja takes dance classes and is already busting out some amazing moves. Keeloni and Dacia seem a little unsure but are willing to give it a try. And Becky is still admiring her hot-pink tutu, and indifferent beyond the fact that she gets to wear it.

I press play on my mashup of "It's My Party" and "Girls Just Wanna Have Fun," and then pass out the party bags with their candy and big black sunglasses—candy for hyperactivity and sunglasses for the perfect look! Then we get started on the dance.

Tanja has so many good ideas; I had no idea that she trains in ballet, hip hop, tap, and jazz! This girl can dance! Stacy has some fun ideas for basic lifts since she's been doing a bit of pair skating. We incorporate her ideas but use two or three people to lift one of us because we're not as strong as a pair boy.

"We should lift Khalli at the very end and strike a pose since it's her birthday," Mila shyly suggests.

Stacy and Yana give each other a baffled look, probably questioning why Mila is being nice to me, but agree with big nods.

"Check out those moves!" Keeloni is pointing to Tanja. "I need to learn how to do that, and like right now!" She laughs as Tanja finishes with a massive fan kick.

Becky decides to try the kick and lands with a solid thud on the deck boards.

"Are you okay?" Dacia squeals before realizing that Becky is actually laughing and not crying. We all bust out in giggles, and Becky reaches over and pulls Dacia down onto the deck boards next to her.

"Oh! That pull and plop move right there, that was a good one!" Tanja snickers with amusement.

"C'mon, guys! Let's start the choreography!" Yana shouts with a fist pump as she suggests a starting pose for each of us.

"Oh wow! It's like coaching an ice show number!" Stacy giggles as Yana puts everyone in their place. "Khalli needs to be in front. It's her birthday after all."

"Nope!" Yana insists. "I have a better idea. Trust me please?" she begs of us.

"I'm in. Let's see your plan!" I offer as she sends me behind everyone so that I'm completely out of sight from the camera.

Yana has everyone pose and then has each of my friends dancing according to their comfort level; how did she figure this out already? She just met them! Becky, Keeloni, and Dacia are doing simple hip bumps, side to side with their hips, while she, Stacy, Mila, and Tanja are really working the dance moves. The four of them split through the three hip-bumping girls like a synchronized skating intersection, clearing an opening for me.

"Come on through, Khalli!" Yana shouts as they create a path for me just as the music sings out, "It's my party." I'm so glad I waited for my friends to choreograph this; they are going to help make it amazing!

CHAPTER 35

Smelliness

We spend another two hours preparing our dance and then record it; this is epic! Even my more hesitant friends are throwing out ideas and dance moves by the end of it. We have four different lifts, some crazy floor spins, Axels by the four skaters, and some really cool kicks! This could not have turned out any better!

By the end, we are exhausted and hungry; that means it's time for pizza and cupcakes! We race inside for pizza, and Dad loads the video on the TV so we can watch our performance while we eat. We literally look like rockstars! Who would have thought a performance on my deck with tutus and sunglasses could have turned out so very amazing!?

"Please send this to me!" Stacy begs. "I would love to upload it online for the world to see, if everyone is okay with that? I can blur out faces if anyone needs me to as well."

My friends message their parents right away for permission. Since it's hard to see our faces with our oversized sunglasses, everyone agrees. I would have never imagined my birthday dance could make us famous!

Mom made me red velvet cupcakes; they are so fluffy and moist! Delicious!

"Let's open the presents while we eat the cake!" Becky exclaims. I cannot wait for you to see your gift. It's actually killing me!" Becky collapses against the couch to prove her point.

"I agree!" Dacia pipes in, but without the exaggerated drama.

How could I possibly argue? I mean, who doesn't like presents?

I open Becky's gift first. It's a customized poster of a skating silhouette in a layback with my name across the top. "This is amazing! I'm definitely hanging this in my room!" I jump up to give her a hug.

Becky grins. "I knew you'd like it! Open Dacia's next. We worked together," she hints.

"You certainly did!" I exclaim as I open a poster frame from Dacia. "Now it will last forever!"

Dacia immediately starts putting my framed poster together as I reach for Mila's gift next. Mila went all out! Unicorn soakers to protect my blades from rust, a velvet scrunchie, and a pair of skating tights with diamonds on them. "Mila! Thank you so much!" I exclaim as I suddenly realize there's still something else in the bag. I pull out a small lump wrapped in tissue paper.

I unwrap it still in the bag and stare with confusion, and then anger starts to build up in me. I really thought we were getting along and becoming friends.

"What is it?" Keeloni asks with a little bit of concern in her voice.

I lift it out of the bag and attempt to set it in my pile of gifts without anyone seeing what it is.

"Deodorant?" Becky's jaw drops. "That's cold!" she sneers, ready to take a stand for me.

Everyone is silent, looking from face-to-face, trying to figure out how to respond. Mila speaks first.

"Your smelliness after class was kind of the beginning of our friendship. But if you didn't work so hard, you wouldn't need it, so I think you should see it as a compliment. It takes a lot of effort to sweat in an ice rink."

Mila's face is genuine. She's not trying to be mean; she's actually attempting to recognize my hard work in a very weird yet somehow thoughtful way. "If you keep working the way you do, I would love to have you reach my level so we can compete against each other!"

"You think I could catch up to you?" I jump up to give Mila a hug, something I never thought I would do. That is an amazing compliment coming from a skater as good as Mila, and I couldn't be more flattered.

"But I do plan to beat you," Mila jokes before breaking out of our hug.

I can't help but laugh; I would expect nothing less from Mila.

Keeloni and Tanja got me movie tickets and gift cards for the concessions. "We loved the last time we all went to the theater together. We'd love to do it again! The concessions gift card is because we know how you love to mix soda flavors."

I can't help but laugh, remembering the last time we all went together.

Stacy and Yana teamed up to buy me my own makeup and brushes. "And this is also a promise to teach you how to use it before your next competition!" Yana smiles.

"Yana will teach you, not me!" Stacy chips in. "She's still doing my makeup for me, but there's no one better to teach you!"

I can't believe how well my friends know me and how much thought they put into my gifts. "I truly love everything! I didn't need presents. I was just so happy all my friends would get to meet each other, but man, do I love these gifts!" I giggle.

"Group hug!" Becky cheers as she races to tackle me! The rest of my friends follow without hesitation.

CHAPTER 36

The Truth

Snuggled up in the tent with our blankets and pillows, it's time for truth or dare. I love this game!

Since it's my birthday, I volunteer to go first. I pick dare; it's always my favorite.

"Ooh! I want to suggest your first dare!" Becky is practically jumping from her seat from excitement.

"Okay, deal!"

"Rudy is home, and I want you to get him for me!" Becky starts.

"Oh, Becky. Don't you remember what happened the last time we pranked your brother?" I ask semi-seriously, but my gaping smile sneaks in and knocks out all concern from my face.

"Whatever you're about to make her do, I'm in!" Dacia giggles.

Becky pauses dramatically. "Okay, I dare you to sneak into his room, steal his pillow for our tent, but leave the pillowcase. You are hereby dared to stuff his pillow-less pillowcase with his dirty socks!"

"*Ew!*" Tanja squeals. "That's a bit mean. I don't support it, but if you use his clean socks, I'm in.

Becky considers for a second and then agrees. "Khalli, I dare you to stuff Rudy's pillowcase with clean socks and then bring me his pillow as victory!"

"Game on!" I sprint up and climb through the tent door, my friends in tow. They follow me to Becky's door, but then Becky holds her hand up, insisting everyone stops.

"It'll be suspicious if we all go in. Khalli, this is your dare and your task alone. Take a picture of the socks in the pillow-case to prove you completed it, and bring us both a photo and the pillow.

I race through Becky's house. No one is home; this will be a breeze! I'm back outside with a pillow in less than two minutes; easiest dare ever!

"Well, that was uneventful!" Stacy jokes. "Now I believe it's your turn, Becky!"

"Um, okay. Dare me!"

"I know!" Mila jumps in.

"Go for it!" Stacy encourages her.

"I dare you to swap your pillow with your brother's new sock pillow and then sleep on the sock pillow!"

"Ugh! No way. That's going to be so uncomfortable!"

"Well, it's your dare," Mila says matter-of-factly.

"Ugh!" Becky groans but complies.

I really like how Mila was ensuring I stay on Rudy's good side even though she doesn't know that he's like a brother to me, so it's okay.

I glance at Mila while Becky runs back to the tent to get her pillow, and she winks at me. I'm pretty sure she actually was trying to rescue me since she doesn't know how close my family is with Becky's.

Becky grumbles as she jogs up to her door with her pillow. She pauses and turns to us as she gives her pillow one last squeeze, as if it had feelings and she'll never see it again.

"Oh, the drama! Get on with it already!" Keeloni giggles.

Becky comes out with a pillowcase full of socks and pouts all the way back to the tent.

"Just be glad I made you change your dare to clean socks!" Tanja laughs.

"Okay, Miss Mila, thief of sleep! It's your turn," Becky says still in full-pout mode.

"I choose truth."

"That's no fun! Who chooses truth?" Tanja asks.

"Well, I'd rather not end up with a pillowcase full of socks, so I do," Mila says with confidence.

"I have a question for her," Yana nearly whispers. This is the least amount of confidence I've ever seen from her.

Mila looks at her, her gaze slightly cold.

"Why did you come to Berger Lake? You hate me, so why would you come where I am?"

Mila pulls her knees up to her chest to hug herself. The tent is dead silent, and it's clear Mila regrets her decision but also feels obligated to answer.

All eyes are on Mila as she wipes the start of a tear from the corner of her eye. Another moment of silence.

I open my mouth to talk; I want to tell Mila it's okay if she doesn't want to answer, but she stops me.

"It's a fair question, one I should be able to answer even if this weren't truth or dare. It's just hard to talk about, but I'll try.

Yana sinks her head; I don't think she imagined there was going to be a story behind it.

"When I was working with Marko Jameson, my skating came to a halt. I didn't tell anyone, but the reason Yana passed me was that I had to take eight months off. I didn't want to stop skating, but my parents had decided to get divorced. When they first told me, I was glad I wouldn't have to hear them fighting all the time. But as soon as my mom moved out, they told me I had to quit skating. How could they make me set aside my dream just because they couldn't get along?"

I swallow. I thought it was rough when I had to take a week off over spring. Eight months?

"Then my mom accepted a new job, one where she would make more money. But it was in Delaware. There's a lot of great skating in that area, so I thought I could move with her. But she didn't want me to come along. She said she needed time to put her life together, but I thought I was her life!

"My dad had been commuting forty-five minutes to work, but since I wasn't skating and my mom didn't need to have a say in where we lived, he decided to move closer to his job in Berger Lake.

"My dad and I got a small apartment. At first I was mad about how small it was, but then I learned he wanted cheaper rent so he could find a way to get me back on the ice. How can I possibly complain if my dad is having less so I can have more?"

Mila continues. "A few months ago, my dad started looking for coaching options secretly behind my back. I loved working with Coach Marko, and he knew I didn't want to make a change. I almost quit skating for good when I found out. But Coach Marko strongly recommended Marie and explained my situation to her. That's why she managed to make time for me in her packed schedule. My dad also took a second job to help cover my skating expenses, so he's never home and never available to give me rides. This is the reason I always take the city bus and need to be at a rink closer to my home.

"I know when we met I said I switched coaches because Coach Marie was better, but I just didn't want anyone to know what happened. I'm sorry I lied. I just wanted to keep everyone out of what was going on in my life. It was like if I didn't talk about it, then maybe things would go back to how they were.

"So anyway, my dad connected with Coach Marie and got me a bus pass so I could get to the rink since he works really late most days. There's no one home, so I'd rather be at the rink than sit alone in an empty apartment. I skate so much because the rink is my favorite place; it feels more like home than our new apartment. When I'm on the ice, it doesn't matter which rink I'm at: the ice is all that matters. When I skate, sometimes I even forget that the rest of my life isn't what I want it to be."

"You're home alone a lot?" I ask. My parents never leave me for more than maybe thirty minutes if they have to run to the store.

"Yeah, but it's an apartment complex, and I know most of my neighbors. So I can easily get to someone if I need to."

"When do you get to see your mom?" Yana asks with concern.

Mila hangs her head, and when she finally lifts it, her eyes are full of tears.

"I don't know. She calls me three times a week: Saturday, Sunday, and then usually Wednesday. But she works so much it's hard for her to call me during the week. I miss her so much. She was always with me before. She'd come to the rink every day and was in charge of all my skating. She helped me with my homework since Dad was always working or commuting. Now I have to do most everything on my own, even make meals most days. I know she loves me, but sometimes I have to remind myself because it's so hard to remember since I never see her. And as much as I love her, I sometimes think I also hate her because she didn't want me to be a part of her new life. It's been almost four months since I saw her last."

All of us stare with saddened eyes, unsure of how to respond.

Mila looks straight at Yana. "And I don't hate you. But I am jealous. You have everything I once had, and I want it again so badly. Your mom is always supporting you. You work with the same coach that you've always had and have an amazing relationship with her. Coach Marie puts in so much effort to make me feel like I belong, but I feel like that's what I am to everyone. Effort. It takes effort for my mom to call me. It's an effort for my dad to keep me skating. It's a lot of effort for Coach Marie to work with me. It's effort for anyone to be friends with me. It's—"

I cut her off. "It's not effort to be your friend, Mila. I really like you and am so glad you came."

Yana and Stacy immediately agree, and the rest of my friends start telling her how amazing her dancing and choreography skills are and how much fun they've had with her.

Mila tilts her head and looks each of us in the eye one at a time. "You guys are my first friends since I quit skating and moved."

Stacy immediately jumps up and hugs her, and within seconds, all of us are wrapped around Mila in one ginormous group hug.

When we finally let go, Mila has tears running down her face. "Don't worry," she mumbles. "These are happy tears. You guys just made me really happy."

We all rush back in for another hug, but Mila breaks free. "I'm not going to be the one to bring this party down! Yana, you asked my question, so it's only fair. Truth or dare?"

Yana smiles boldly. "Dare. I always pick dare."

Mila giggles. "I think I'll do the same next time!"

We all laugh, but secretly I can't help but feel so bad for Mila. She's starting a whole new life and doing it without her mom to help.

"I know!" Keeloni jumps in. "You're a figure skater! I double-dog dare you to do a double Axel."

"Okay!" Yana says nonchalantly as she calmly walks out of the tent.

We all follow eagerly as she picks a flat spot on the lawn.

"Ready?" she asks over her shoulder.

"Good luck!" I call. I know how hard my Axel was to land. This is quite a feat. I know she's been working on them on the ground, but I haven't seen her land one—and now to do it under pressure!

With next to no effort, Yana jumps up into two-and-a-half rotations with what looks like a clean landing.

"Whoa!" we all cheer.

"When did you learn that?" Stacy asks. "It looks fully rotated!"

"I started working on it off-ice right after the ice show. Coach Marie checks it every week to make sure I'm making the proper corrections. It's about a quarter rotation short still, but she said my positions are strong enough that it's ready to put on the ice. We actually started last week in the harness at Carnival Ice Center."

"Now I really am jealous of you," Mila says, but instead of in a mean way, she speaks in a tone of voice that suggests Yana should be proud of herself.

"Thanks!" Yana smiles, clearly catching the compliment from Mila.

I love that we are all getting along; I finally have my rink family back!

Before we wrap up truth or dare, Becky eats a bug, Keeloni climbs a tree, and Tanja tells us who she's crushing on: I would have never guessed she secretly liked Gio!

Stacy, since she's a little bit older, told us all about her first date and how he spilled soda all over her at the movie theater when he tried to nonchalantly put his arm around her. Her entire date sounded like a complete mess; she said she never went on another date with him again! And Dacia, who always picks truth, picked a dare! We made her ding-dong ditch my parents, who never came to the door—probably because they could hear us laughing outside of the window. Guess that joke was on us because we hid behind the bushes for about five minutes waiting.

CHAPTER 37

Eleven

At 8:00 p.m., Stacy and Yana have to go. Yana's mom is picking them both up and dropping Stacy off on the way home. Stacy is taking over for her sister as a babysitter for the night; they split the shift so that Stacy could come to my party.

I love that my friends made arrangements in their schedules to come spend the day at my birthday party! I imagine Yana will be tired for her early morning lesson tomorrow, and that Stacy lost out on some babysitting money; it means so much that they are here!

"Hey, everyone! Let's get a group photo before Yana and Stacy have to leave. I want to remember today forever!"

"Like you could actually forget!" Becky jokes.

She's not wrong, but I do love photos!

I race into the house to get Mom for the picture. Dad's in the kitchen and offers to take the photo for us, but I can only laugh at his offer.

"Just because I almost always cut the heads out of the picture doesn't mean it won't be great!" he jokes. "It will be a fantastic work of art, focusing on the feet of your friends."

"Thanks for offering, Dad," I reply as sincerely as possible, "but I don't really need pictures of my friends' shoes to remember my birthday."

"Someday you might regret not having a photo of their shoes! What if today's shoe trend becomes historically famous? Then what!?" Dad calls after me as I jog up the steps to find my mom.

Mom comes without hesitation when she hears that Dad wanted to take our picture. "Don't let him. You'll be holding still for hours before he finally gets a good photo! This is why there are very few photos of you and me together other than our selfies. We are missing body parts in every one of his photos, mostly half our heads. I don't understand why it's such a struggle for him, but at least he owns up to it." Mom says, making sure Dad is in earshot of her as she picks on him.

Dad huffs at her jokingly as I hand her my phone to take our picture.

When we get outside, my friends are in the process of creating a human pyramid. "Climb on top, Khalli!" Mila shouts from the bottom of the pyramid. "But please hurry, this is heavy!"

I don't hesitate to climb on my friends' backs, slowly making my way to the top. "Why are you moving so much?" I screech, holding onto their shoulders for dear life!

"Because you're moving!" Becky hollers back, glimmers of pain radiating through her voice.

Keeloni starts laughing as I climb over the top of her. "That tickles! Get your foot off my foot!" she calls between giggles.

"*Ah!*" I shift my foot and continue my climb.

"As soon as she's at the top, please take the picture, Auntie Krista!" Becky begs. "This is so much harder than I thought it would be!"

"I'm at the top!" I shout as my hand misses Dacia's shoulder and lands on her head.

"Argh!" she grunts as she strains to hold her place.

"Hurry! Take the photo!" Becky yells.

"But I'm busy recording the climb!" Mom laughs, indifferent to everyone's suffering. "Okay, smile!"

We all make smile noises. *Eeee* fires out of my mouth, as I force a smile while squeezing my core muscles to maintain my balance over the wobbling pyramid.

"Okay! I took about a dozen. Come on down!"

"How?" Dacia and I shout at the same time.

"From the top down," Stacy directs.

I start climbing down just as someone collapses on the bottom level. "Whoa!" I holler as my body tumbles downward on top of Dacia and Tanja.

"Ugh! You guys are heavy!" Becky pushes her way out of our pile. "Good thing that was only three levels tall, or that would have hurt!" She brushes her pants off like she was just tackled in a football game.

"Hey! I fell from the top. What are you complaining about?" I joke.

"You fell on top of me! You're lucky it's your birthday!"

"Is everyone okay?" Mom asks with concern.

We all nod and say we are. It was a relatively gentle collapse thankfully.

"Good, because I got that on video and would feel bad watching it over and over to laugh at you all if someone actually got hurt!"

"Show us now!" Becky squeaks, and we all huddle around Mom to watch both the climb and the fall. We all groan as we watch ourselves crash into the ground.

"I'd love to see that again," Yana exclaims.

Mom presses play again as we all squeeze in even tighter. The closer my friends tuck into our huddle, the more content I find myself feeling. How lucky am I to have this amazing group of friends? I can't believe how blessed I am that all my friends made time for me on my birthday, and that they've all finally met each other and everyone gets along.

I stop watching the video and instead look around at each of my friends and their hilarious reactions. I have to be one of the luckiest eleven-year-olds in the world! I could not have asked for a more wonderful birthday, or for a better group of people to spend it with. Something tells me eleven is going to be an amazing year! I wrap my arms around as many of my friends as I can.

"Group hug!" I exclaim. And the biggest, best group hug ever is exactly what I get! I couldn't possibly be any happier than I am right now…

About the Author

At the age of ten, Allye Ritt began a figure skating hobby that would eventually turn into a lifelong career. Allye is now a seven-time US Figure Skating Gold Medalist, an International Dance Medalist, and has also achieved the Skate Canada Gold Dance test. She has skated professionally around the world on three different continents and currently coaches full-time as a career. She is a Master Rated Coach through the Professional Skaters Association and also serves as the director for an area figure skating program. Allye thoroughly enjoys guiding her students as they grow in the sport of figure skating and loves watching their confidence blossom as they excel.

In her free time, you will find her in an ice rink, reading, at the gym, or spending time with her husband, Jeffrey, as well as their cat, Tatyr. As a former middle and high school teacher for German and history, Allye holds a deep passion for learning, especially about historical and modern cultures. This passion has led to a genuine desire to see as much of the world as possible. Together, Allye and Jeffrey love travelling and taking in new places and experiences whenever they have the opportunity.

Printed in the USA
CPSIA information can be obtained
at www.ICGtesting.com
LVHW040306050923
757091LV00004B/496